PROVIDENCE

BY THE SAME AUTHOR

The Debut (A Start in Life)
Look at Me

PROVIDENCE

PANTHEON BOOKS NEW YORK

ANITA BROOKNER

All rights reserved under International and Pan-American Copyright
Conventions. Published in the United States by Pantheon Books, a division
of Random House, Inc., New York. Originally published in Great Britain by
Jonathan Cape Ltd., London, in 1982.

Library of Congress Cataloging in Publication Data.

Brookner, Anita.
Providence.

Reprint. Originally published: London: J. Cape, 1982.

I. Title.
PR6052.R5875P7   1984   823'.914   83-19449
ISBN 0-394-52945-6

Manufactured in the United States of America
First American Edition

PROVIDENCE

O N E

Kitty Maule was difficult to place. She had a family, that was known, and she disappeared every weekend, so it was assumed that she lived in the country, although her careful appearance belonged to the town. When asked about her background Kitty usually simplified, for her family history was perhaps a little colourful. She found it too tiring to recount, for so much additional explanation was needed, footnotes on alien professions, habits, customs that most people could not be expected to understand and which were to her as native as the colour of her own hair. She usually said, 'My father was in the army. He died before I was born.' This was the exact truth, but it was not all the truth, for the father to whom she delegated the prominent role in her family history had never even registered in her consciousness as absent. Quite simply, he had never been there. Her mother was there, and her grandmother and grandfather; they would continue, long after their own deaths, as parents, racial memories, a certain kind of expertise, a certain milieu, untouched by their almost accidental mingling with the conventional life of an English wartime marriage. Yet Kitty felt herself to be English; hence her explanation, 'My father was in the army'. And indeed no one had ever faulted her on grounds of Englishness. Yet she felt a part of her to be shrewd and watchful, mistrusting others, paying less attention to their words than to the words they were not voicing. She thought these characteristics were a sign of some moral defect, and always hastened back to her life's work of establishing the true and the good and perhaps the beautiful, of believing the best of everyone, of enjoying what life offered, not lamenting what it withheld. This, in fact, was how her father had been.

Her mother, Marie-Thérèse, remained the little French girl whom her parents destined for a good marriage, even though that marriage had come and gone some time ago. Marie-Thérèse was the eternal *pensionnaire*, homeloving, conventual, quiet, and obedient to those strange parents of hers, Kitty's grandparents, who so consistently undid the myth of Kitty's Englishness, in which she believed so fervently and which no one who knew her sought to disbelieve. She had two homes: one, a small flat in Chelsea, where she kept her father's photograph, taken on his last leave; the other, her grandparents' house in the suburbs, where, once inside the front door, one encountered the smells, the furnishings, the continual discussion that might take place in an apartment house in Paris or perhaps further east. An air of dimness, of stuffy comfort, an emanation of ceremonious meals, long past, an airlessness, hours spent on the routine matters of rising and eating and drinking coffee; an insistence on food, the centrality of food; great sadness, organizing the simple empty days, but never despair, never the complaint known to English doctors as depression. But sadness, much sadness. When Kitty went back to her other home, the rational little flat in Chelsea, it seemed to her quite empty of everything, of smell, taste, atmosphere, sound, food. She would look out of the window for signs of life, not realizing that she never did this in her other home, in the suburbs, where her grandparents lived. Occasionally a shout would come from the pub on the corner, but it seemed to her that even there very little was going on. And on these Sunday evenings she would survey the empty street, vaguely disquieted, longing to be one thing or the other, for she felt that she was not what she seemed. She looked enquiringly at the photograph of her father, whom she thought of as 'Father'. Her grandfather she called Papa and her grandmother Maman Louise. They called her Thérèse, the name she resumed when she went back to them. Away from them, she was Kitty. And most of the time she felt like Kitty. Not all the time, but most of it.

Her father, John Maule, had died, but her grandparents, her mother's parents, had monstrously survived him and had taken the widow and her child back into their care. And here the strangeness began, for they were not like other people, and destined perhaps to designate the island of remoteness in Kitty's character which gave her so much trouble. Her grandfather, Vadim, a Russian whose family had drifted to France in the early years of the century, had originally been part of an acrobatic act which, after some years of touring the provinces, and worse, village fairs, market days in outlying regions, reached the high point of its fortunes with an engagement at the Olympia Music Hall in Paris. One evening, after the performance, while eating his supper in a small brasserie with his two brothers, who were the rest of the act, Vadim met and fell in love with a bold-looking yellow-haired girl who was evidently enjoying a night out with her friends. They had been to the Olympia and had recognized the brothers; they showed no trace of shyness and, with red chapped hands, raised their glasses in only slightly mocking tribute. Soon they were all sitting together, toasting each other properly in a *fine*. The girls were seamstresses from the rue Saint-Denis, and Louise, the one with the yellow hair, had ambitions for the future. There were fortunes to be made in the dressmaking business, she said, and she planned to go to London, where a sister of her father's lived, and to set up on her own there. As the goodnight shouts died away in the frosty street, Vadim knew that he would desert the act and go with her. Why not? It was an easy decision to make.

They married, went to London, and found a couple of rooms in Percy Street. Life was not easy, but Louise was clever and determined. She began as an outworker, but was soon making dresses for private clients, which Vadim would deliver, springing through the London streets on his acrobat's legs. Soon there was a little girl, Marie-Thérèse, whom Vadim wheeled about in her pram and whose cheeks were caressed by the various traders and shopkeepers in the district. A warm roll or a piece of fruit would be slipped into her small hand; she would eat it carefully at home, listening to the sounds of her mother's sewing machine, dreamy, and idle, and capable of sitting for hours without moving, quite unlike either of her parents. Louise worked day and night, her bold clever eyes now shadowed with fatigue. 'Come, Marie-Thérèse,' Vadim would say, 'let us think of a good hot dinner for your Maman.' And Louise would take ten minutes off and eat the dinner that the little girl had pretended to help to cook. 'Thank you, my pigeon,' she would say, inclining her face for a kiss. Then she would go back to her machine and work far into the night.

For Louise and Vadim, the high point of their lives was not the birth of their daughter but their triumphant installation in the salon in Grosvenor Street. Louise now had as many clients as she could handle, and Marie-Thérèse was more used to the company of the girls in the workroom than to that of her own mother. Yet both parents were intensely proud of her. She was so quiet, so gentle, so graceful; how, they wondered, in their hard-working lives, had they managed to produce something so exquisitely and apparently useless? They dressed her in black, with a little white collar (very chic: Louise had made the dress with her own hands) and trained her to be a receptionist in the salon. They had sent her to a French school, and her manners were charming and formal. Louise's clients became very fond of her.

One day, Captain John Maule, newly commissioned, accompanied his sister Barbara to a fitting for her wedding dress. He sat awkwardly on a small gilt chair and admired the thin neck and wrists of Marie-Thérèse, although he was secretly appalled by her mother. Louise seemed to him large, hoarse, and coarse; he had never seen such obviously dyed yellow hair and he watched in spite of himself as the ash fell from her cigarette holder on to the bosom of her dress. She was clever, she was knowing, she was tired; Barbara Maule flushed with annoyance as Louise pinched the fold round her waist, pulled down the neckline of her wedding dress, grimaced, then pulled it up again. Yet she bore it uncomplainingly, for she was not an attractive girl and she knew that Louise would make her look her best.

When Marie-Thérèse was given leave by her mother to go out to tea – for Louise was trying to sever any connection between her daughter and the workroom – John Maule followed her. He came again and again with his sister to the salon, and eventually presented Marie-Thérèse with an engagement ring. They were married on his embarkation leave. Louise made her daughter's wedding dress, sitting up all night to finish it. It was of the palest pink china silk: an audacious choice destined to set off her daughter's delicate white skin. Instead of a veil, there was a little pill-box hat. It was the most beautiful wedding dress Louise had ever made.

She and Vadim dressed their daughter for her wed-

9

ding as if she were an expensive customer having a final fitting. Vadim, on his knees, regularized the folds. Louise, her cigarette holder put aside, pulled down and smoothed the narrow sleeves. After fifteen minutes of complete silence – for Marie-Thérèse was in a dream of her own – Vadim sat back on his heels. '*Ça y est*,' he pronounced. Louise, her arms crossed, stepped back and viewed her daughter. A rare smile broke up her grim features. She stepped forward again and lightly pinched Marie-Thérèse's cheeks, to give her some colour. '*Ça y est*,' she agreed, and with a brief final pinch on the chin, added, '*Vas-y, ma fille.*'

Marie-Thérèse and John Maule went to the coast, out of season, for their honeymoon. They walked endlessly, hand in hand, talking about their respective childhoods. They were in fact like two children who have elected each other as best friend. At night they slept soundly in each other's arms and woke in the morning with the ease of youth. He was twenty-one, she was eighteen. At the end of their holiday, which was also the end of his leave, she saw him off at Victoria and then went home to Grosvenor Street and her mother and father. She never saw John Maule again, for he was killed shortly afterwards. She gave birth to a baby girl – Catherine Joséphine Thérèse – nine months after her wedding day.

The shock of Marie-Thérèse's bereavement affected them in different ways. Vadim was the only one who cried, his fine-featured brown face creasing in spontaneous spasms of grief. Louise worked steadily on, every night, sketching and smoking and coughing. She let the yellow dye fade from her hair and went white; when her daughter brought the child to Grosvenor Street on her weekly visit she said little but her pouched clever eyes missed nothing. She saw that there was something wrong with Marie-Thérèse's pallor and when the doctor diagnosed anaemia and a heart murmur she was not surprised: her sister Berthe had been the same. She installed a series of refugees and displaced persons in the innocent little house in the suburbs that John Maule's parents had given their son and daughter-in-law as a wedding present, and when the child was old enough to go to school she bought a larger house in Dulwich, and converted it into two flats. The child would come into John Maule's small legacy when she was twenty-five. Until then, she must stay at home with her mother.

Marie-Thérèse showed her daughter the beautiful pale pink wedding dress and said, 'When you are ready, Maman Louise will make one for you.' Then she pressed her hand to her side, as she so often did these days, and murmured that she was going to have her rest. 'Maman Louise,' cried the child in Grosvenor Street, 'will you make my wedding dress?' 'Yes, my pigeon,' said Louise, 'and Papa will make the cake.'

'Vadim,' she said to her husband after these visits. 'How long can this last? She makes no effort to marry again. She sits at home with the child who is clever and will want to go out into the world. What is to be done about Marie-Thérèse? And I need more petersham for Miss Herbert's skirts – you will have to go to Mortimer Street. This New Look is exhausting. The girls in the workroom complain. I could kill Christian Dior.'

But she went on, producing the crinoline ball dresses for which she became famous in the 1950s. She derived a contemptuous satisfaction from subduing the noisy exuberant debutantes who bought her dresses for their first season into some semblance of demureness. Only the advent of the miniskirt seriously disturbed her. London was suddenly filled with young and outrageous girls, like the rue Saint-Denis of her youth. The bales of satin, taffeta, and organza, the buckram for the hip padding and the whalebones for the strapless bodices of the ball dresses were suddenly obsolete. Louise's hair was snowy white, her face creased into folds, her eyes screwed up against the smoke of her cigarette. Vadim seemed not to have aged by a single year. He was as small, as lithe, as brown as he had been the first time she had seen him on stage at the Olympia. He did all the housework now, as well as running the errands. He was a familiar figure in Soho, in his beret and his soft-soled shoes, springing along as if in training.

Yet they were older and they felt it; they could no longer keep up. When the debutantes discovered Nepal and began to go off in Land Rovers, they decided they had had enough. After Louise's heart attack, they pensioned off the girls in the workroom, sold the remainder of the lease, and went to live in the upper part of the house in Dulwich, to be near Marie-Thérèse. There Louise sat and smoked, against doctor's orders, and played patience and read through her piles of *Vogue* and *l'Officiel*. Vadim, quieter now, made excursions to the shops and did the cooking.

It was a bizarre and anomalous family. To Kitty, who loved England as only one who is not wholly English can do, Louise and Vadim and Marie-Thérèse were almost an embarrassment. They sent her away to school and as she struggled to come to terms with her fellow-boarders, who were confident and energetic and kind and who invited her home in the holidays, she was almost glad to be anonymous and unplaceable, although she regretted not having known her father, whose fading photograph was on her mother's bedside table, and felt a pang when she thought of the pale pink wedding dress. Returning home from these visits, she found she needed several days to change over from being Kitty to being Thérèse. Vadim, an enthusiastic cook, would put plates of food before her at odd times, urging her to taste his latest creation, which was usually both pungent and idiosyncratic. Gradually the comforting monotony of

12

school dinners faded from her memory. Louise would assess her grand-daughter's graceful figure, and lively pallor, and nod her approval: she would carry clothes well. Marie-Thérèse, whom widowhood had restored to virginity, moved slowly about the little flat, watering her plants, reading the romantic novels to which she was addicted and which Kitty sometimes borrowed. Music was listened to, on the radio which Kitty had bought them with her first allowance, Vadim assessing the beat with a stern and critical hand, the muscles of his legs flexing automatically. He was in their flat for most of the day, doing odd jobs for 'my girls'. Louise, upstairs, played patience. They ate together, since it was simpler that way, speaking French, the bottle of wine ritually recorked at the end of the meal, salad eaten from the same plates as the meat; much bread. Marie-Thérèse found Papa's cooking too rich and gasped with discomfort. '*Petite nature*,' said Louise, not unkindly, sticking her fork into an apple and turning it round and round to peel it.

Two years before she came into her father's money, Kitty moved into a home of her own. Both Louise and Marie-Thérèse encouraged her to do this, although Vadim was mournful. She found a tiny flat in Old Church Street, near the river in Chelsea, filled it with second-hand furniture of no great value, and worked at her research – for Louise was right and she turned out to be clever. But she went home at the weekends, and sometimes, as she came out of the station, she would see Vadim, in his Basque beret and his tennis shoes, pinching the fruit at the greengrocer's to see if it was ripe, smelling the fish at the fishmonger's, and demanding to taste the cheese. Part of her cringed with the imagined antagonism of the shopkeepers. Part of her admired his tenacity. Part of her wished her English father were alive. Yet another part noted what fashion magazines

13

were on sale, and bought them for Louise.

To the family she was like a marvellous foreigner. 'You know, my darling, there is no need for you to study so hard,' said her mother. 'I should like you to get out more and meet more people.' She did not say where, for she did not know. Vadim unpacked her basket, inhaling with ecstasy the freshly ground coffee that she bought for him. Louise was mostly interested in her clothes. 'Off the peg?' she would say, incredulously. 'Off the peg? *Mais tu es folle, ma fille.* I can still make you a dress that you would not find anywhere in London. Vadim, fetch me that piece of silk jersey in the bottom drawer.' So Kitty would spend most of her weekend in her petticoat while Louise made her a dress and Marie-Thérèse watched or listened dreamily to the radio, her place in her novel marked by a handkerchief. After their dinner they would all watch television together, for Vadim and Louise followed the various serials with great intensity, like children. Marie-Thérèse tired quickly but felt obliged to sit up with them, vaguely moved by the absorbed expressions on her parents' faces. 'I can't see much happiness there, can you, Papa?' she would say, or, 'You were right, Maman, she is after his money.' *'Belle fille tout de même,'* Louise would murmur, her eyes narrowed, as if taking measurements. They went to bed early, for Kitty yawned with boredom at the end of her day, and when she retired to her small room she would take one of Marie-Thérèse's novels, being unable to face the books she knew she should be reading. Those books were waiting for her in Old Church Street. Her subject was the Romantic Tradition.

She applied for and got a research appointment at a small but richly endowed provincial university, famous for its departments of History and Microbiology. She was immediately noticed because of her exquisite clothes. 'Milady Maule,' observed the head of depart-

14

ment's secretary. 'Must be rolling in it.' Thus are reputations falsely made. In a few months the head of department's secretary said to her friend, 'If she can afford to go to Paris for her clothes, I wonder why she bothers to fill in time here.' At the time when this remark was made Kitty was in Chelsea, disposing of a damp and overfilled sandwich pressed into her basket by Vadim who thought she needed a little pick-me-up after her journey home. The smell hung disagreeably about her hands, and she washed them several times before getting down to the Romantic Tradition. The transition from one life to another was not always easy.

After Marie-Thérèse's death, quickly and quietly one evening at the dinner table, the old people became older and seemed to revert to their less illustrious days in Paris, before success had brought them their modest affluence. Louise's dress was now dusty with ash; her swollen feet were stuck into slippers. Vadim did not bother to remove his beret in the house. Only when Kitty came, at the weekends, did he indulge in his vigorous and haphazard cooking: soft-boiled eggs greeted her when she arrived, longing for coffee, and cups of soup, rocking in their saucers, broke up the afternoon. She swallowed it all down for she was terrified of hurting him still more, and found it difficult to endure the long day sitting with Louise, whose eyes were now dull and vague. She asked them questions about the past in an effort to animate them, for she remembered them as the liveliest people she had ever known. All Louise would say was, 'If only she had married again!' 'But Maman Louise, she is with Father now,' said Kitty, her voice sounding as false to her as had the prayers she had murmured at school. Louise would shrug and an expression of pity would pass over Papa's face, as if only now registering the fact that his grand-daughter had been affected by an alien and sentimental culture. In his world, and that of Louise, you had your youth and your energy and your determination. Nothing else was given to you, but all could be taken away. As it had been.

Gradually Kitty came to dread the weekends which were symbolized for her by the food thrust lovingly in front of her. She began to refuse it and her heart ached as Vadim, dejected, bore it away again. They spoke little, her attempts at cheering them up proving fruitless. They were waiting for news and she had none to tell them. Occasionally Louise, energized by a strange kind of malice, would stir from her semi-permanent doze, would open her eyes, survey Kitty from head to foot, and question her. 'Well, *ma fille*, where are your lovers? Who will take you home tonight? For whom do you wash your hair? And your studies, will you ever finish them?' Turning her puffy hands in her lap in a strange mute appeal, she said, 'I do not understand your life. Are your colleagues real men? Is it so different here? What do you discuss over your tea and biscuits? Come,' she would say, with a glint in her eye, but the hands still turning, sadly, 'come, *ma fille*, tell me about England.'

T W O

When dining alone, Kitty Maule tended to dispatch the meal as quickly as possible and also to distract herself from the actual business of eating. She found it helpful to balance a tray on her knees rather than to sit down forlornly at an empty table, and to read, listen to the radio, or even sometimes to wander about, as if only lending herself to the task of digestion. The vagaries of her appetite had increased since her mother's death, at dinner, some three years earlier. It had been a strange and peaceful death, her mother collapsed in her chair, one small hand trailing through some fragments of walnut shell. The faintly sour scent of her grandmother's discarded fruit peel was still in Kitty's nostrils, as well as the sight of her grandfather, with tears pouring down his face, crying, 'Marie-Thérèse! Marie-Thérèse!' Somehow the event had been incorporated into their family life, but Kitty Maule could never sit down to a hearty plateful of food without hearing the plaint, 'Marie-Thérèse! Marie-Thérèse!' Her throat would close and a faint trembling would start in her hands. People had given up asking her out. She was better off at home, where she could concentrate on feeding the birds with the crumbs from her plate. Sometimes she was perfectly all right, as now. Sometimes she ate with enjoyment, as when she prepared a meal for her lover, Maurice Bishop. But when she was alone, there hovered faintly in the background of her mind the memory of the hand and the walnut shells, and the cry, 'Marie-Thérèse! Marie-Thérèse!'

On an evening such as this, a Friday, she made an omelette and ate it carelessly, wandering about her little kitchen, absently waving her fork. In her mind she was going over her last conversation with Maurice, who had telephoned earlier and thus both calmed and unsettled her. She would see him, officially and discreetly, at a lecture the following week; she would sit in the audience with all his other admirers while he discoursed on the cathedrals of England, for, although an historian by profession, he was also a romantic and devout Christian, a strange combination which appeared to keep him perfectly happy. His dispositions and predispositions manifested themselves in a series of public lectures which regularly filled the main theatre of the small provincial university lucky enough to retain him as its Professor of Mediaeval History, although offers were continually coming from Oxford, where, it was predicted, he would take up his next post. His devotion to the cathedrals of England, on which he offered a series of inaccurate but moving insights (with slides), entranced his audience and enraged the Roger Fry Professor of Significant Form who writhed in his seat but was forced to attend through sheer pressure of public opinion. 'Charismatic shit,' he was once overheard muttering to his wife. 'Sanctimonious bastard. How does *he* know what Canterbury was supposed to look like? I suppose he'll get Durham sorted out next. Is there no end to this?' 'I thought it was lovely,' said his wife, clapping stolidly, along with all the other ladies, the Friends of the University, the departmental secretaries, the retired librarians. 'And anyway, he comes to your lectures on Cézanne. You can hardly do

18

less than return the compliment.' 'Oh yes, he casts his nets wide, does our Maurice,' agreed the Roger Fry Professor. 'Nothing human is alien to him. He really feels at one with those simple mediaeval masons.' 'Oh, shut up, David,' said his wife, adding, fatally, 'You're jealous, that's all.' After which, they said nothing to each other for the rest of the evening.

Kitty Maule, dressed in her best, although Maurice could not see her, would watch the handsome smiling figure mounting the steps to the platform, and try not to sigh as he surveyed the image on the screen before turning to his audience, his hands on his hips, his legs and buttocks braced as if for sexual activity. He was a beautiful man and everyone was faintly in love with him. Kitty herself had loved him for two years and had entertained secret hopes. But their brief affair had settled down into a strange comradely routine which puzzled her but which she accepted. She accepted his random telephone calls, too random for her taste, and his eventual reappearance at her dinner table, where he would talk about his work and eat her food appreciatively; and seeing him there, she too, at last, would eat.

Tonight was Friday, she would see him on Wednesday, and the following Monday he would come to dinner. She would have little chance of talking to him on Wednesday for he was always surrounded by eager questioners after his lecture, and indeed these occasions made the university so popular that the head of the Romance Languages Department, who was also the Dean, arranged small sherry parties which sometimes went on quite late. One these occasions the Friends of the University, who were also the wealthier ladies of the surrounding countryside, paid homage, their fine diamond rings glinting on hands weatherbeaten with gardening. She could hardly go up to him and ask him what time he would arrive at the flat, nor would he bother to let her know, so she could only nurse her glass of sherry in a corner, watching him being charming to the Friends, and calculate when she could buy the meat and whether or not to prepare something that would only need reheating or whether to do something fresh on the night and therefore easier in terms of forward planning but more difficult in terms of realization.

From these preoccupations she was sometimes rescued by the jovial figure of Professor Sir Hamish Redmile, the Dean, two years past retirement but showing no signs of retiring, wearing a Vaughan Williams hat to indicate his status as an elder of the university tribe. He had earned his title by serving on a Royal Commission whose recommendations had never been heard of again. He was a tireless fund raiser and enjoyed these occasions, since he did not intend to leave the university until his great project – the New Building – was formally established. Sir Redmile, as the Roger Fry Professor called him, treated university life as an endless series of significant little social gatherings, at which contributions might eventually be raised. He appreciated Maurice Bishop not only for his scholarship, his presence, his popularity, and the fact that he had not yet defected to Oxford, but also for his background ('impeccable'), his family home in Gloucestershire, his mother's title, and Maurice's private income. He also, in a lesser way, appreciated Kitty, who was doing research work for him and giving a useful number of seminars. She too, he was given to understand, had an income of her own, and indeed she wore such exquisite clothes that he supposed the income to be large, although it was not. 'My dear Miss Maule,' he would say in a noble and enveloping tone of voice, 'were we not privileged this evening? To have the fabric of England brought to life in such a way! And,' he raised a conspiratorial finger, 'you and I are going to feel even more at home next year.

I hear our dear Maurice is planning a series on the cathedrals of France.'

Kitty knew about Maurice's project. Even while she typed out his notes on the cathedrals of England, she knew that the cathedrals of France would follow. Indeed, Maurice had mentioned the idea at dinner one evening and had become more and more enthusiastic, getting his maps out of his briefcase and plotting his route on her kitchen table. He would take the car, he thought, and spend the whole of the Easter vacation driving from one site to another. Of course he could only concentrate on the major monuments: Laon, Rheims, Chartres, Bourges, Le Mans, Amiens, Rouen. 'It will be a lot of work,' said Kitty, 'and it seems a pity to do only the big ones. Normandy is full of very pretty minor cathedrals. Coutances. Evreux.' She had been there on holiday once and had spent long rainy days taking refuge in churches, whiling away the afternoon by reading her guide book in the dank and aromatic aisles, waiting until she could, with a good conscience, have her afternoon cup of chocolate in the nearby pâtisserie. 'Troyes,' mused Maurice. 'Saint-Urbain. Very extraordinary church, that. Too florid for my taste, actually. I prefer the early and undecorated.'

Kitty preferred the later and the more exuberant. She liked evidence that some life was actually stirring in the stone and felt a sense of dread in the darker and more ancient of churches, where iron heels rang out pitilessly on flagstones and the candles burned more brightly in the gloom. She always lit one, for Marie-Thérèse, but she felt nothing, for she had no sense of Marie-Thérèse's presence in her life and therefore did not believe that the dead could live eternally. She kept her scepticism to herself, paying respect to Maurice's unquestioned beliefs, nourished on certainty, she thought, but none the worse for that. All the better, in fact.

21

Her main preoccupation was whether Maurice would ask her to go with him to France. She would be useful, she knew, could do all the boring things, while he got on with driving the car and getting from one place to another and being inspired by what he saw. French, after all, was her mother tongue; she could save him a lot of time and trouble. But how to suggest this? The suggestion must surely come from him, and he was still bent over his maps, his hand blindly reaching for the cup of coffee she had poured for him. It seemed as if he could take the cathedrals of France without any human company to dilute them, his passion for the absolute, for God and beauty, sustaining him where she herself would have counted the hours on her own and calculated the moment at which she might have crept out to the pâtisserie. She felt humbled by the comparison between them, as always; he was finer, larger, better than she was, his insights nobler, his whole fabric superior. With his background, I suppose, she thought vaguely, imagining spacious lawns and grey stone and summer afternoons and his impeccable mother receiving guests.

Although anyone who saw Maurice and Kitty together would have thought them a charming couple, she would have been remarked upon as the luckier of the two, lucky to attract such a man as Maurice. Both were tall and graceful, but there the comparison ended, with their silhouettes. Kitty was artfully put together, manufactured and tutored by her grandmother in the way of presenting herself advantageously, given the names of shoe designers and handbag makers and a special price because of the trade connections. She felt exhausted sometimes by the sheer effort of composing her appearance, and not always sure of the results. Was she perhaps too elaborate? Maurice was ineffably natural. He wore fine clothes, but carelessly, handmade shirts without a tie, cashmere pullovers instead of jackets. She had first seen him drinking tea in the Senior Common Room at the university, a place where low armchairs housed many spreading bottoms and stomachs clad in grey flannel or beige tweed, where legs could be seen protruding in maroon socks and ginger suede shoes, where blouses and shirts gave off the dingy glare of nylon. Kitty, alarmed by her first entrance into this important place and dressed as her grandmother decreed a lady should be dressed, instinctively felt drawn to the tall figure wandering around with a cup in one hand and a saucer in the other, a signet ring just visible on the finger beneath the saucer, his brown hair – the hair of a formerly blond child – curling behind his ears and on the nape of his neck. That day he had worn a white shirt, with a red pullover, narrow grey trousers, and black leather mocassins. He had swung round and greeted her with a pleasant vague smile, the smile she had come to know so well, and because she was not yet afraid of him she had responded naturally and they became friends. They both lived in London and commuted to the university, which was strictly against the rules, and this created a further bond between them. Very occasionally he gave her a lift back to town and it was during one of these late evening drives that she had fallen in love with him.

That had been two years ago. Since that time, his smile had become no less pleasant and no less vague, for however much she pined for him she knew that she was not indispensable to him. And at bad moments, when she woke in the night, she knew that she was not even necessary. She congratulated herself on her ability to hide her feelings, unaware of the fact that the Roger Fry Professor's wife had observed to her husband, with some satisfaction, 'Well, she doesn't appear to be getting anywhere with him. Trying too hard, if you ask me.'

On the evening with the maps she had moved quietly round him, only too happy to have him in her kitchen, and willing to forgo even the cathedrals of France if only she could be sure that he would come back to her. As he plotted his course, with his diary in one hand, she permitted herself to gaze at his fine head, since he could not see her doing so. The longish brown hair, the skin healthy with the country air of his weekends at home, the clear green eyes, and the delicate ivory ears filled her with longing and delight. There was so much that she wanted to ask him, but she knew that with Maurice questions never met with answers. He remained formal and pleasant, but he disarmed her easily. She wanted to know if he ever thought about her (but she supposed not, for he was always busy) and anyway, to ask that sort of question was unimaginable. But if he took her to France, that would be a sign, and moreover a sign that the world would see, a sign that her grandmother would welcome.

He straightened up, hands on hips. 'You ought to come with me, Kitty,' he said. She turned away from him, to hide her trembling hands. 'Why not?' she said, after a minute, and with no particular inflection in her voice. 'My dear child,' he laughed, stretching out a long arm and resting it on her shoulder. 'You know perfectly well why not. Just think of your reputation.'

This was his way and it confused her. She did not know whether, in his world, it would have been truly scandalous to contemplate such a journey with a woman not merely of marriageable age but of marriageable intentions. He was, after all, such a very superior person and it was typical of him to remain untouched by the inconclusive character that sometimes attends such episodes. Her being an orphan, she supposed, made him feel more responsible for her reputation, and he did not know that if only she could be seen to be with him a little more obviously, her reputation would be made for life.

Since that time he had continued to talk about his projected trip to France but had never again suggested that she should go with him.

And since that time their evenings together, and they were not very frequent, for during the term Maurice was greatly in demand, had filled her with a slight but persistent melancholy. From the moment at which she sat down to wait for him, to the moment some four hours later when she heard his car roar off into the dark and sleeping street, she was not certain why she could no longer respond with that unforced pleasure she had felt in the Senior Common Room on that first afternoon. She could still see him as she had seen him then, the fine vague smile, the polite manners that made him come forward to greet an obvious stranger, the glint of his ring beneath the saucer. It seemed to her, in retrospect, the best moment of her life: her recognition of him, her ease in welcoming whatever would come of it. Since then there had been intimacies, but he always left her afterwards, and she had had to try very hard to censor out of sight a feeling of dismay, almost of shame. For she never knew when she would see him again.

She had thought that he might guide her towards some conclusion, and because that conclusion had been so long delayed, she wondered if she herself might be too pressing and urgent in wanting it, pressed and urged by the need to justify herself in Louise's eyes and to bring happiness to those grandparents whom she had so far disappointed. Although she knew that she was threatened – by their eventual death, which would leave her alone and undirected – she felt that she was at fault in failing to make some vital connection with Maurice's desires and intentions, and when she thought this she was in despair, for how could she put right what her

25

very ignorance had put wrong? She tried to read his mind, to follow his thinking more closely. She saw there something inaccessible. The vague, pleasant, and somehow mysterious smile closed her out, while closing in something highly significant, something that she did not know, something foreign to her. Tell me about England, she thought. She was tormented by rumours of a broken engagement in his past, for who would break an engagement to Maurice, and might it not be repaired? Once, in desperation, she had surmounted all her scruples and mentioned this casually to her friend Pauline Bentley in the Romance Languages Department.

'Didn't you know?' said Pauline in surprise, and proceeded to tell her the story. Maurice and this girl had known each other since childhood. Lucy something or other. They had always known they would get married. Apparently they were the most beautiful couple and it was to have been the wedding of the decade. But Lucy something or other had been a bit unstable, had had religious doubts, with none of Maurice's certainties, and two months before they were due to get married, she had broken off the engagement. Some sort of breakdown, apparently. She had then announced that she was going out to Calcutta, to work with Mother Teresa. Which was where she was now. Maurice had taken it surprisingly well.

'Merde, alors,' was Kitty's immediate and uncensored reaction to this and she was so ashamed that she felt herself blushing hotly, as if she had been discovered in some major indiscretion. Since that time she had tried to be as pure and as noble as Maurice himself, for she now understood his unwillingness to commit himself after so great a disappointment. The news about Lucy had made her feel better (knowing that she was behind bars, as it were) and a great deal worse, for how could she compete? She began to search herself for any seeds of

26

faith that could be cultivated, for she now saw that the key to Maurice was his belief in the divine will. Or the divine purpose, if that were the same thing. Something divinely sanctioned, anyway. In her own soul she found nothing, only the weariness, boredom, and fear that had afflicted her in those churches in Normandy, where the candles guttered and the obtrusive footsteps of the faithful sounded confidently behind her. She could not in all faith go to church but sometimes she picked up her mother's Bible, for she believed that it contained the answers, if only she could ask a disinterested question. Which she could not. But one day she found a passage that seemed to have a message for her, purely for her. '*Il m'a envoyé ... pour proclamer à ceux de Sion qui pleurent, que la magnificence leur sera donnée au lieu de la cendre, l'huile de joie au lieu du deuil, un manteau de louange au lieu d'un esprit affligé.*' She was so strangely moved by this announcement that she sought it in the Authorized Version, as if doubting its authenticity in the language of her own family. And there it was, more splendid, more resonant, more authoritative, as if God's native tongue were English: ' ... beauty for ashes, the oil of joy for mourning, the garment of praise for the spirit of heaviness.' She read no more, for everything else seemed irrelevant.

Beauty for ashes. She sat in her kitchen in Old Church Street, her plate washed up and put away, the crumbs for the birds strewn on the windowsill. She allowed her fears and griefs to come to the surface, in the timid hope that it was now safe to do so. Some day, unless a miracle took place, she would spend all her time in this kitchen and it would become her permanent and only home, instead of the temporary staging post she had always thought it might be. But this was too dangerous to contemplate, and she turned her head aside, to the window. It was a quiet evening. It was always a quiet evening, for there were few passers-by at this time of day. The only sound was that of an insistent radio, from the flat of her neighbour Caroline, the divorcee. Across the street she could just see the publican's wife, one hand fluffing out her blonde hair, taking the air on her doorstep before opening time. Kitty tried to imagine what Maurice was doing, and failed. She tried to remember the assurance of the words in Marie-Thérèse's Bible. She did in fact remember that there was a staff meeting on the horizon, that she had a lecture to prepare – on the Romantic Tradition – and that in a week's time she had to give a seminar, about which she had mixed feelings. Her subject was *Adolphe*, a short novel about failure. She did not care for it much, and worried about her ability to convey its quality.

As she moved, with the heaviness of a much older woman, from the table at which she had been sitting, the telephone rang. It was Maurice. 'Are you in London?' she asked in some surprise, for she had imagined him taking off for home. 'Yes,' he said mildly, 'I quite often spend the weekends here. I rang up about Monday. I can't make it, I'm afraid. My mother's coming to town.' Kitty laughed, though she felt panic. 'It's Monday week, you idiot. Didn't you write it down?' 'Oh, fine,' he said, 'fine. I'll see you then.'

After that she leaned out of the window for a bit, trying to get her thoughts into order. He had telephoned. He was coming. That was the thing to remember. Anyone could get a date wrong. In a little while she felt calmer, her life-line re-established. Then she got out her notes and began to work.

T H R E E

Oddly enough, she had never found her work difficult. On the contrary, it appeared to her in the guise of a neutral element in which there was no need for subterfuge, for watchfulness, or even for desire. Work, to Kitty, was something you did, not something you talked about. Her neighbour, Caroline, who had come down in the world, had often regaled her with stories of her fascinating past and would end such reminiscences with the words, 'I really ought to write a book.' 'Why don't you?' Kitty Maule would ask, with genuine curiosity. She felt that the wish was father to the thought, and that no one need be without an occupation. Beauty, of course, offered its own dispensations: beautiful women, by a rule she acknowledged but did not understand, were somehow allowed to do nothing of worth and yet to command the time and attention of others. Kitty preferred her busy life, which she characterized as an easy life spent doing difficult things. At least, she supposed they were difficult. In fact, it took her more time to cook a special dish for Maurice than it did to write a paper or prepare a seminar. Yet she took no pride in the fact of doing such work and refused to think of it as important. Quite simply, it gave her no trouble and therefore she took no credit for doing it.

'My God, Kitty,' said Pauline Bentley, in the Romance

Languages Department. 'You don't know how lucky you are. I use work as a weapon against depression. I see it as a way of outwitting nervous illness. You'd be surprised how many people feel this way.' As she said this she combed her hair viciously, for she was ashamed at revealing so much. Yet Pauline was a superb lecturer, polished and impeccable, and for this reason much admired by the students. With less desperation behind it, Kitty's style was milder and more popular. She enjoyed her intellectual obligations and did not sense them as onerous. Secretly she regarded her task as a temporary and rather pleasant way of filling in the time until her true occupation should be revealed to her. She did not quite know what this was but she sensed that she would rather excel at duties other than the ones with which she had occupied herself over the last few years.

They were in Pauline's room, preparing to go to a staff meeting. Pauline regarded these meetings, which took place once a term, with undisguised contempt. Kitty, on the other hand, rather liked them. As an occasional teacher she was grateful for the opportunity to attend, and although she could not always understand what was being discussed, she managed to look alert and even took notes. Her zeal, which was genuine, had been noted with approval by Professor Redmile. 'I wonder if he'd notice if I marked a couple of essays,' mused Pauline. 'I tell you, Kitty, when I get to hell I expect to find a perpetual staff meeting in progress.' She took a miscellaneous bundle of papers, which did indeed include a few essays, from her desk, and set off down the corridor. Kitty followed demurely in her wake.

The meetings were always held in a gloomy and oleaginous brown room, which had been a dining room when the building had been occupied, in baronial state, by the benefactor of the university. Professor Redmile sat at the head of the table that gleamed with a curious

30

icy veneer in the bad light; at his side, importantly, sat his secretary, Jennifer, taking the minutes. They filed in reluctantly – the historians and the linguists – Dr Martinez, Professors Gault and Bodmin, Mme de Marcoussis, Mrs Vogel, Dr Oliphant, the Roger Fry Professor, whose hapless task it was to teach French art to the French Department, Italian to the Italians, German to the Germans, and still try to maintain some sort of autonomy, and last of all, Maurice Bishop. In front of every seat was a pencil and a pad of paper. With one accord, as Professor Redmile welcomed them at the start of a new term and looked forward to soon being able to give them some definite news about the New Building, all picked up their pencils and started drawing, a defensive move intended to drown out the hearty delight in Professor Redmile's voice but one which gave them the appearance of a rather retarded occupational therapy class. Kitty, all innocent attention, watched the Roger Fry Professor incising a deep jagged abstract on his pad. Mme de Marcoussis favoured a delicate shading, involving ceaseless motion with the pencil. Professor Gault always drew an Archimedes spiral. Once, at the end of the meeting, Kitty had stolen round the table after everyone had left to see what Maurice had drawn: a flying buttress.

To Kitty, who lacked extensive diversion, these occasions were ones of pure entertainment. They also gave her an opportunity to look at Maurice, if he were within her line of sight, and to savour the extreme delight of anticipating their next and more private meeting. Her expression was always rigorously schooled and she was discreet in a way that would have been becoming in a nineteenth-century governess; nevertheless, the Roger Fry Professor, looking up unexpectedly from his cubist design, had once noticed her look and was thus in possession of her secret. She had not seen him, but the

Roger Fry Professor had noted with an inward sigh that his wife had been right and that Maurice had made another conquest. His dislike of the man was becoming unmanageable. Maurice, all delicate attention to what Professor Redmile was saying, was not aware of any of this.

Maurice, thought Kitty, will you not look in my direction? I am only here for your sake. I do not, I confess, care about the New Building, or even believe in it. I am fond of all these people, even of Professor Redmile, but if you were to vanish and they were to remain I cannot think that I should stay here long. You have done so much for me. You have made me believe in what I am doing, whereas I really only started it as a sort of hobby; since knowing you, I have tried harder than I would have normally, and I have done better than I thought I could. And they are pleased with me; that is a new sensation for me. I find this work easy because in a way I am doing it for you. I want to be excellent, for you. The fact that Pauline is quite openly reading an essay – a fact noted by Jennifer; the fact that the Roger Fry Professor is once again demonstrating that he can knock off a respectable drawing in the manner of Delaunay; the fact that Mrs Vogel is making out her shopping list: all this delights me because we are in the same room and sharing the same experience. I shall remember a day like this, although you will not. You have more important things to remember. Will you not meet my eye?

But Maurice, with his pleasant smile, only leaned over to Jennifer and slipped a small note into her hand. Blushing, she looked at it, then, rather more slowly, handed it over to Professor Redmile.

Kitty, her hands idle, had seen Jennifer's change of expression, and resolved sternly never, ever, to look like that. She switched her thoughts to the Romantic Tradition, with which she was supposed to be eternally preoccupied, and wondered if it really existed. Could one build a tradition out of a series of defiantly autonomous individuals, all of them insisting that what they felt had never been felt before by any human being? They were an impressive but disheartening lot, she always thought, coming so rapidly to maturity, haggard with experience by the age of twenty-five, and somehow surviving their own disastrous youth into a normal life-span. Even an abnormal one: look at Victor Hugo. Except, of course, Gérard de Nerval. He was central to her thesis, for he did not survive. She did not know what she found more impressive: the ability to stagger on through a life exaggeratedly devoid of normal happiness, or the ability to admit a radiant fragmentation of the mind that would put one out of the struggle altogether. What worried her was that there appeared to be no middle way. She could not accept that so much ardour and longing, so much torment and courage, should peter out into the flatlands of middle and old age. And anyway, where did the Romantic Tradition end? Easy enough to decide when it began, and even how. But did it, terrible thought, still persist? Might she have started something that might prove to be more extensive than she had originally supposed? Might the Romantic Tradition outlive her desire to have anything more to do with it?

As usual at these meetings, an extremely complicated change of timetable was being proposed, for no very good reason other than it gave them something to have a meeting about. Instead of a straight historical run through the syllabus, an elaborate schema, referred to by Professor Redmile as a four-tier structure, was to be substituted for a period of one year to see how the students adjusted to it. 'They will turn up anyway,' said Pauline wearily. 'The only difference is that they will not know exactly what they are turning up to.'

'If you will refer to the outline which Jennifer has very kindly prepared,' said Professor Redmile, 'I think you will see, Dr Bentley, that this proposal has a great deal of virtue in it. The students will gain a more exciting historical perspective by being brought up against different periods in unexpected conjunction. Perhaps you will all study the outline and give me your views?'

Pushing aside their drawings, they bent their heads obediently over the sticky and unevenly photocopied sheets which represented their tasks for the coming academic year. There was a minute's concentration, followed by a unanimous absence of comment. The silence was eventually broken by Maurice, who said, 'If you adopt this scheme, Hamish, you will have the Dark Ages one morning and the Enlightenment the next. That is a conjunction to challenge even the most sophisticated student.'

They laughed heartily, delirious with boredom. The Roger Fry Professor ground his crepe-soled orange shoes together in a mixture of fury and despair: Maurice had just destroyed his chance of getting his lectures done by Christmas instead of having to give them all in the summer, when everyone stayed away. Professor Redmile, graciously joining in the laughter, gave a signal to Jennifer to have the tea brought in, and with that the meeting was to all intents and purposes over, although the talking was about to begin.

Tea and biscuits at the staff meeting were, for Kitty, the high point of an otherwise socially unadventurous week. She smiled with genuine pleasure as she accepted her cup; it was the only sort of party she enjoyed these days. She dressed with extra care for these occasions, at which she said nothing; she thought her amateur status entitled her merely to attendance. She was exactly the sort of person Professor Redmile liked to have around.

34

She knew this and it gave her added pleasure. The scene had, for her, a strange exoticism: the hideous room, the north light, the dull atmosphere, compounded of the smells of cigarette smoke and sheets of photocopied paper, the muted and rumpled appearance of everyone except Maurice and herself, the enormous amount of luggage they managed to bring in – bags, briefcases, mackintoshes – the ceremonial plate of chocolate biscuits handed round by Jennifer's assistant, all this seemed to her stranger and more desirable than the home life of her grandparents with their variants on normal dress and erratic impromptu meals. It was on these occasions, ridiculed by her grandmother, that she felt that she had a definite if modest status, in a context which did not take into account her beginnings or her background, a context, moreover, which contained Maurice. To be at one with him, even on so tenuous a basis as this, seemed to her a factor which could not but have a bearing on the rest of her life.

She watched him covertly over the rim of her cup. He was talking to Professor Gault, a tiny, weary man who was an expert on Ariosto. Maurice was asking some question which Kitty could not hear, for the exchange of views, which had been noticeably absent during the meeting, now threatened to become vocal and even noisy. She watched Maurice's fine hands, describing some parabola, shaping some outline – she could not hear what was being said and she strained slightly, then caught herself doing so, and consciously relaxed – and Maurice's face, alight with enthusiasm and energy, as he made his point, whatever it was, seeming to have found the answer to the question he had been asking, for Professor Gault merely nodded, and when Maurice had finished talking, they both laughed. I wish he would look at me like that, thought Kitty with longing. Are we so civilized, so controlled, so expert in our concealment that we are never allowed to reveal anything to the world about ourselves and each other? She looked down quickly at the sticky brown table, for she could feel her contentment ebbing away, felt it suddenly to be nugatory, laughable, a pretence that her rational self could not accept. She dreaded these moments, which came without warning, and waited with distress until they should have passed, leaving her once again in possession of her secret.

It was almost dark in the gloomy room, and in that moment before the lights were switched on, she thought ahead in panic to her return home, with its docile routines that she longed to bring to a violent end. Her sedulously careful rituals for outwitting the long nights, the exorcism of her various familiars and dreams, were losing their virtue and their ability to soothe her. And yet, she thought, I have so much to look forward to; at least, I have next Monday. Perhaps it will go well, better than I have ever dared imagine. Perhaps I can reintroduce the subject of the cathedrals of France. Perhaps I can initiate some sort of change for the better. I cannot stand it, she thought suddenly. I cannot stand the waiting and the carefulness. It should not be like this. And, immediately, she suppressed the thought.

The Roger Fry Professor, noting the alarm in her eyes, got up and switched on the lights. Then he sat down again, heavily, beside her, and asked, 'How does this fit into the Romantic Tradition, Miss Maule?'

Kitty thought. 'Impossible to imagine. Romantics never consult others on their plans and behaviour. They are always performing for an unseen audience. Spontaneously. Erratically. Oh, I suppose Chateaubriand attended many meetings, but one thinks of him, with his chair turned aside, brooding, and making notes on the folly of recent history. He was not a man for the barricades.'

'I am,' said the Roger Fry Professor, surprisingly. 'I think you have to be. There comes a point at which it is no longer wise to do nothing.'

Kitty turned her eyes away from Maurice and considered this.

'Do you really think so?' she asked. 'What about that wise passiveness we are always hearing about?'

In the corner of her line of vision she could still see Maurice's dark blue pullover, and she wondered if it were new – she had not known him to wear it before. But she kept her eyes on the Roger Fry Professor's permanently red, permanently hurt face, and wondered if he were right.

'Wise passiveness gets you nowhere,' he said. 'By the way, do call me David. Wise passiveness gets you left behind. If I hadn't been so wisely passive a moment ago, I could have got all my lectures over by Christmas. Instead of which I shall have to plough on through the summer when everybody with any sense is sitting on the lawn.'

'But David, you know there wasn't the slightest chance of the timetable being changed. This proposal is put forward at least twice a year. It's a way of giving Jennifer something to do. And Professor Redmile loves the idea of upheaval. You remember when he wanted to move the library from the basement to the second floor? No one could think of any reason for stopping him, especially as the librarian wasn't at the meeting.'

'Yes, how did that one end?'

'In a compromise, I think. Someone suggested a new date-stamping system, and he let it go at that. They never got round to it, of course.'

He nodded thoughtfully. 'But that is still not an argument in favour of wise passiveness. Wise passiveness is a front. It means you don't do any work.'

'The Romantics, of course, were compulsive workers,' said Kitty. 'Reams of memoirs, acres of painting, hours of music. They liked to pretend it all came to them in a flash. I find that rather fine, that assumption of effortlessness. It's a pose, of course, but it has a certain elegance, you must admit.'

Her expression lightened, for she had found the key to her difficulties, and a pointer to future behaviour. An assumption of effortlessness. Whatever it cost her. The elegance of a behaviour calculated to disarm, never to give offence. No apparent pain. The dandyism of great endeavour combined with a gracious ease of manner. Like a Stoic. Like a Romantic. Why, she thought, in some surprise, they were both. She turned to the Roger Fry Professor and smiled. 'Thank you, David,' she said. 'You've given me an idea for my lecture.'

'That may be the first time an idea has ever come out of one of these meetings,' he replied, and smiled reluctantly as he saw her face, pleasant and composed once more, as he wished it to remain.

A burst of laughter from the other end of the table signified that the meeting was getting out of hand, had in fact ended some half an hour ago. But now, paradoxically, no one was willing to leave, except Pauline, who was shoving her arms into her cardigan, her pencil held between clenched teeth, her pile of marked essays stacked beside her. Kitty looked round her once more with appreciation. It had been quite a good afternoon. Even if these bad moments came – and she did not know why they should – she would deal with them by means of her new strategy of smiling them out of the way. A strategy of elegance appealed to her, for although it was a way of giving the lie, it was also a way of cherishing the truth.

Her expression, alert and tender with contemplated possibilities, swept round them once more and this time her eyes encountered those of Maurice, who smiled at her. She smiled back, but did not allow herself to linger over the pleasure of seeing him look at her in this way. Instead, with beating heart, she turned back to the Roger Fry Professor, and said, 'I like your drawing. But why do you always do the same one?'

'Ah, that is called stylistic mastery. In years to come, young men at Sotheby's will look through their portfolios and say, "Yes, a typical example". It may surprise you to know, Kitty, that I despise a great deal of non-representational art. Have you realized that it is very easy to practise something you despise?'

'I hadn't thought about it. In that case, why not despise lecturing in the summer? You'll sail through the whole term.'

Again, out of the corner of her eye, she could see Maurice noting down something in his diary, and wondered what it was. But her face was still resolutely turned away from him, and she knew that there was no point in her trying to speculate. It was, moreover, not elegant.

'I long,' said the Roger Fry Professor, 'for the unqualified admiration of the multitude. I want to be borne from the rostrum and carried aloft in triumph. I want them to believe me as they once believed Savonarola or John Knox. But above all, I want them to turn up in droves and to fight for their seats. In the summer, most of them are sitting on the lawn doing their revision and making plans for their holidays.'

'I didn't know you enjoyed lecturing.'

'I hate it. I am frightened to death every time. My wife thinks I am an idiot. But I contend you have to be an actor to do it well. Like Maurice Bishop.'

She smiled at him quite calmly. 'I don't know about that. I quite enjoy it myself. Although I must confess to being nervous about this public lecture on the Romantic Tradition. It's by way of being a test, I think. If I pass the test, I am no longer on probation.'

He nodded. 'I can see that. I'm surprised that you enjoy it, though. You seem to me to be too honest to go for that kind of pleasure.'

'It's the only time I ever really forget myself,' said Kitty. 'Real life seems to impose such insuperable problems that it is quite restful to think about something entirely different and for which I take no responsibility. I did not cause the Romantic Movement, after all. It is not my fault. And no one is going to accuse me of perpetrating it on the rest of the world. It is like the war. I am not guilty. It happened, but I was not there. There is a marvellous freedom in that, don't you think?'

'Do you feel responsible for everything else?' he asked.

'Oh, yes,' she said. 'Yes, I do.'

But they had no time to discuss this further, for briefcases were being snapped shut and chairs vacated. Someone shoved open a window, to air the room, and there was a sudden draught as the door swung wide. Knocking on the table with a heavy glass ashtray, Professor Redmile attempted to halt their move away from the meeting. 'One moment, ladies and gentlemen,' he said, as they half turned back to where he was still seated, at the head of the table. 'One moment. Jennifer has an announcement to make.'

They looked over their shoulders expectantly. Jennifer cleared her throat, blushed scarlet, and announced, 'Fire drill will be on the second Wednesday of term. Please see that you know who your fire officers are and where the hydrants are placed.'

'Hear, hear,' said the Roger Fry Professor, and with that they were free to go.

F O U R

To Kitty's resolutely professional eye, *Adolphe* was mainly interesting for its conjunction of eighteenth-century classicism and Romantic melancholy. If she concentrated on this aspect of the story, she could overlook its terribly enfeebling message: that a man gets tired of a woman if she sacrifices everything for him, that such a woman will eventually die of her failure, and that the man will be poisoned by remorse for the rest of his life. She decided to ask her students to analyse the use of words, and to dedicate the last half-hour of her class to a wider investigation of Romantic accidie. She feared that her students might become sentimental on this point and was mainly interested to see if they had any views on it that she had not encountered before.

These students were three in number. 'Larter, Mills, and Fairchild,' said Professor Redmile. 'Larter an obvious First. Mills, as you know, older than the other two. I understand that he is on a year's sabbatical from some teacher training college. Miss Fairchild quite promising but obviously not up to the standard of the others. Miss Fairchild will need a little cosseting, Miss Maule. I know I can count on you.'

They were indeed a very disparate group, hardly a group at all. John Larter, the obvious First, was a disruptive influence but a very necessary one. Painfully

41

thin, excited and excitable, unshaven, anxious to please, chain smoking, irritating, and, Kitty recognized soberly, after she had known him some weeks, a kind, honest, and potentially brilliant scholar, the rarest thing in the world. He would settle down if given the right scholarships, the right fellowships; his filthy jeans and sweater, which did not suit him, for his whole demeanour was too anxious, too adult, too wary, would eventually give way to something more conservative and presentable; he would have his wispy hair properly barbered; he might even learn to withstand the blandishments of the elitist life he would be called upon to live, and thus maintain the extraordinary purity of his intellect. For at the moment there was no mystification in him. That would come later, with public success. If life tripped him up, on the other hand, failed to provide him with those essential opportunities, he would go all the way down, ruin his health, drink too much, make do sadly with substitutes. 'What did you do in the vacation?' she had once asked him. 'Well, I was going to Grenoble to do my Stendhal stuff,' he had answered. 'But I met someone on the train and got off when he did. You know how it is.' He had flashed her a smile that was both malicious and wistful. She feared for him, but recognized that she could do nothing to help him. She was a restraining voice when his words threatened to spin out of control or run out of sense; she restated the position for him, enabling him to start again after a wrong direction too energetically pursued. At the same time, she marvelled at the profundity of his thought, the generosity of his ideas. Theirs was in fact an ideal alliance. He made her feel like a teacher. She did not make him feel like a student.

Philip Mills had disconcertingly grey hair, which made Kitty unsure of her role. He was a teacher himself and some years older than she was, kind, polite, cautious, bifocalled. She wondered if he were satisfied with his year off, or whether he found them all disappointing. Not Larter, surely? For Mr Mills was a good foil to Larter, argued with him, was irritated by what he called his free association, was given to unseemly exasperation, which he had surely never been able to express so freely. 'What do you *mean*, tragic? How can a word be tragic in itself? It can only have tragic implications.' 'It can have a tragic sound,' Larter would cry and immediately produce a flood-tide of tragic-sounding words. 'You have lost the point *again*,' Mills would answer testily. 'You always go past it. Your analyst has got a lot to answer for.' At this stage Kitty would intervene; sometimes it would take her a couple of minutes to impose her will on their perfectly valid disagreement and restore a sense of unity to her class. She enjoyed these episodes, for she possessed a sense of fairness, and was happy to see them chattering amicably a few minutes later, or when they bundled their books together at the end of the seminar and went off for a cup of tea. She was on excellent terms with both of them.

Not so with the troubling Miss Fairchild, who had never been observed to open her mouth unless invited to do so. When Miss Fairchild read an essay, it ran quite sensibly for about seven minutes, ending with a complete sentence and a full stop. Then Miss Fairchild would lift her limpid eyes to Kitty and say, 'I'm afraid I didn't have time to write any more.' There would be no answer to this. For she was so extremely beautiful that it seemed a concession for her to have written anything at all. Even Larter was half hypnotized by her. She had long pre-Raphaelite tendrils of beige hair with which she played throughout the seminar, drawing them back briskly behind her neck as if in preparation for some sort of announcement, or winding a lock round and round her fingers and across her lips, her immense eyelids lowered in obviously meaningful reminiscence. Her skin would retain its even golden character throughout the extremes of heat and cold experienced in Kitty's little attic room; the greenish eyes would watch unblinkingly as Larter and Mills went for each other. She usually wore a cotton skirt and a dark blue jersey, borrowed from a brother, Kitty supposed, for its sleeves nearly covered her hands. Her full and rather low bosom occupied most of the front of it.

By mutual and unspoken consent, the two men left her out of their discussions. But Kitty, who was obscurely unsettled by her speechless presence, made sure, like a good hostess, that her questions were regularly addressed to Miss Fairchild. When thus addressed, Miss Fairchild would clear her throat, uncross her legs or shift her position in a sensuous fashion unsuited to the occasion. She would sometimes answer quite reasonably but was clever enough to let Larter run away with her argument, which he did without even noticing he had been activated. At such moments Miss Fairchild would give a faint smile, push her hair behind her head, and then let it fall forward, shielding her face. Kitty was rather frightened of her. She recognized that Miss Fairchild was unteachable, and this in itself was frightening. But more than that; Miss Fairchild was unteachable because she felt she knew enough already.

'Will you describe to me,' said Kitty calmly, 'some of the *tristes équivoques* of which Adolphe accuses himself?'

'In fact,' said Larter, 'there is no equivocation there at all.' He took a massive drag on his eighth cigarette. 'Adolphe decides to seduce this woman, then grows tired of her, and wants to return to a more suitable way of life. She hangs on. His weakness in the face of her suffering is not equivocation. It is cowardice.'

'But Adolphe himself calls this suffering something

44

else. And he is in a state of conflict. Hence, *équivoques.*
Look at the words and trust them more. After all, this is
Constant's story, not yours. And a novel is not simply a
confession, you know. It is about the author's choice of
words.'

Mills pondered. 'He never uses the word *amour*.'

'Yes, he does,' said Kitty, 'but he is talking about love
as a phenomenon, not about his love for this particular
woman. I am sorry to hammer this point but you must
take notice of how the words are handled, in which
context they are used. They will tell you everything. For
her part, Ellénore considers Adolphe *misérable*. What
do you make of that? Miss Fairchild?'

Miss Fairchild raised her startling eyelids and smiled,
to herself rather than at the question, as Kitty feared.
'Well,' she said, very slowly, 'this woman is a nuisance.
She's old and she's foreign. She's ruining his career.
Obviously, she's being unfair.'

Kitty, trying to control her annoyance, said, gently,
'That's not quite what I meant. None of these words is
used accidentally. The word *misérable* is used because
there is a great deal of shame involved. How do we
know this?'

'The preface,' said Larter excitedly.

'All right, the preface. Some think that this is the most
important part of the book, although it was added some
years later. Ten, to be precise. I think it might be useful
if we were to translate the preface at this stage. Into the
exact equivalent; no flourishes, please. Mr Mills?'

Mr Mills donned his bifocals. '"I wanted to depict the
malady suffered by even the most arid hearts on account
of the sufferings they cause, and the illusion that leads
them to suppose that they – "'

'"That these sufferings",' murmured Kitty.

'"That these sufferings are lighter or more superficial
than they really are. From a distance, the image of the

sorrow one causes appears vague and confused, like a cloud easy to pierce; one is encouraged by the approbation of an entirely artificial society, which replaces principles with rules and emotions with ... "'

He stopped.

'*Convenances*,' said Kitty. 'That's a difficult one, isn't it? Yet that is perhaps the most crucial word in the paragraph.'

'Conventions?' supplied Larter.

'I think so. We'll see. Go on, Philip.' She always called them by their Christian names when she got carried away by the argument. She felt a closeness with them, then. Even Miss Fairchild was watching Mills, although her hands were now hidden in the sleeves of her pullover.

'" ... which replaces principles with rules and emotions with conventions, and which condemns scandal as tiresome, not as immoral, because it ... "'

'Society,' said Kitty.

'" ... because society is quite accommodating towards vice when there is no scandal attached; one feels ... "'

'"It is felt ... "'

'"It is felt that attachments which have been made without reflection can be broken without any harm being done".'

'Remember that sentence,' said Kitty. 'That is what the novel is all about.'

Mr Mills, quite unmoved by what he was reading, looked over the top of his glasses and asked her if she meant him to go on. Kitty indicated that she did.

'"But when one sees the anguish that results from these broken attachments, the painful astonishment of a deceived soul, that defiance ... "'

'Mistrust,' murmured Kitty.

'"That mistrust that succeeds perfect confidence ... "'

'"That mistrust that succeeds perfect trust",' said

Larter, in wonder, with an expression of pain.

At least one of them is getting there, thought Kitty, and aloud she said, 'Take that sentence again, please, Philip.'

'"But when one sees the anguish that results from these broken attachments, the painful astonishment of a deceived soul, that mistrust that succeeds perfect trust, and which, forced to direct itself against one being out of the whole world, spreads to that whole world, that esteem driven back on itself and not capable of being re-absorbed, one feels, then, that there is something sacred in the heart that suffers because it loves; one discovers how deep are the roots of the affection one thought to inspire without sharing it; and if one overcomes what one calls weakness, it is by destroying in oneself all that was generous, by tearing up all that was faithful, by sacrificing all that was noble and good. One stands up after such a victory, which is applauded by friends and acquaintances, having condemned to death a portion of one's soul, tilted at sympathy, abused weakness, and outraged morality by taking it as a pretext for harshness; and one survives one's better nature, ashamed or perverted by this sad success. This was the picture that I wanted to paint in Adolphe".'

They were all silent for a moment. Even through the clumsy translation they had felt the writer's sadness. And his skill. Kitty drew a deep breath.

'Now, Jane,' she said. 'Do you still feel that you can dismiss Ellénore's use of the word *misérable*? It doesn't mean miserable, remember. It means wretched. Wretched as in poor. One of the early meanings of *misère* is poverty.'

Miss Fairchild smiled. Kitty decided to take this for assent. She cleared her throat.

'We are in fact talking about a particular state of bankruptcy,' she said. 'And although the novel is

written completely without imagery, in the driest tradi-
tions of the eighteenth-century moral tale, it lacks the
buoyancy and optimism of the eighteenth century. Has
it acquired anything that would have been unthinkable
in the eighteenth century?'

'Despair,' said Larter.

'All right,' said Kitty. 'What sort of despair?'

Larter took off his glasses, rubbed his eyes, and for
fifteen minutes gave them an almost seamless account of
the Romantic dilemma. This, according to Larter, but in
fact according to Chateaubriand, was due to the col-
lapse of moral standards in the Revolution, to the
repudiation of the supernatural, to the deconsecration
of the churches and the exiling of the priests, to the
attempt to live according to the humanitarian rules of
the eighteenth century, to live without piety and belief
and consolation. But God, having been lost, was difficult to find again. Romantic man, man without God,
had to behave existentially, and experienced isolation.

'Yes,' said Kitty. 'Romantic man has lost his original
unity and uncovered a new complication. Even in the
eighteenth century they knew that this might happen.
Mme du Deffand asked Voltaire what he proposed to
put in the place of the old beliefs, you remember. She
sensed trouble ahead.'

Mr Mills then objected that Existentialism could not
be projected backwards into the nineteenth century.

'Yes, it can,' said Larter. 'Existentialism is a Romantic
phenomenon.'

He then gave them ten minutes on Existentialism.

'You may be right, in general,' said Kitty. 'But we
have not yet reached the concept of the Absurd. The
hero of *Adolphe* experiences pain through his conscience. He does not explain it as a general rule. What
we have here is a moment of supreme morality. I would
refer you once again to the words.' She looked down

48

at her text. '*Imprudences. Règles sévères. Faiblesse. Douleur profonde.* I am, at the moment, picking these up at random.' Under the table she glanced at her watch. 'For next week, will you please bring a full list of such words. I think we shall arrive at a better understanding of the Romantic dilemma once we have them in front of us. That will do for now.'

She closed the book in front of her, feeling pleasantly exercised. Such afternoons, once the initial nervousness had passed, gave her no trouble. She felt that she had left her onerous daily self behind, and with it all problems of nationality, religion, identity, her place in the world, what to cook for dinner, all thoughts of eventual loneliness and illness and death. She passed, at such times, into a sphere of pure meaning, derived from words written nearly two hundred years ago, and those very words, used for her enlightenment, did in fact enlighten her.

Mr Mills took off his bifocals and put them back in their case. Larter stretched and yawned. The air was blue with smoke and stale concentration. Miss Fairchild released her hands and closed a notebook in which she had not made a single note. She never did.

Kitty Maule, her manner and gesture precise, wished them good afternoon and waited until they were out of earshot. With their departure came silence, a friendless silence. I am not old enough for this way of life, she said to herself, and wondered why this had occurred to her. She would have liked to join them, to go on arguing, to have walked to the bus-stop with Mills and Larter. Ideally, she would have liked to travel home with someone, with Maurice, to be precise. She did not like going home. She did not like waiting on the station platform with the lights blurring in front of her tired eyes, her mouth stale with the taste of tea from the station buffet. She never managed to read on the train.

On this particular day, at that dwindling hour between five and six, she was tired enough to allow herself to feel quite seriously down-hearted. She took a taxi at the other end with a sense of defeat, not of earned relaxation. As she put her key in the front door she wished there were someone inside the house. At the same time, she had to be pretty deft to avoid her neighbour Caroline, the divorcee. Caroline, always available for a chat, thought that others should be too. Caroline's door would open seductively, and she would say, 'Oh, Kitty, I'm so depressed. Do come and talk to me.' 'Just hang on a minute, Caroline,' Kitty would say. 'I must dump these books. I'll ring you later.'

Once inside her own flat, she put on the lights and telephoned her grandmother to see if she were all right. Papa answered the telephone as usual; she could hear the television in the background, blasts of sycophantic laughter, gales of applause. They always had it on too loud. And Vadim never told her exactly how things were. Everything was always for the best in the best of all possible worlds; Louise had had a good day, rain was forecast for tomorrow, so take an umbrella, they had had marvellous onion soup for lunch, and it was so easy to make – would Thérèse like him to come over and make some for her? The work of an instant, no more. No? Of course Louise was, well, a little tired, perhaps, but they were not so young, my darling, you must expect this. What was she going to eat, he asked, and waited for the answer, enthralled. Kitty, who intended to have something on toast, told him that she would have a chop and some salad. Never neglect the vegetables, said Vadim passionately. And the cheese. Not too much coffee. She agreed. 'Can I say goodnight to Maman Louise?' asked Kitty, to cut him short. There was a pause, the dropped telephone picking up the sounds more clearly, then a creaking of footsteps, heavy steps, then a heavy breathing. Well, *ma fille*, said Louise, a good day? A good day, said Kitty. You wore the blue? Yes, agreed Kitty, she had worn the blue. Hang it up immediately, advised Louise. With pleats one can never be too careful. And tissue paper in the shoes, of course. Always, Kitty said, don't worry, I always do as you say. Louise let a pause elapse, pregnant with disbelief. Then, goodnight, my pigeon. Sleep well. Until tomorrow.

When Kitty replaced the telephone the silence was complete. It was such a very quiet street, she thought. She had always disliked those stories which begin, 'In the town of H——, in the province of O——'. They seemed to shut her out. The action of *Adolphe* takes place *'dans la petite ville de D——'*. Such a refusal to give the story its usual complement of detail turns it into a sort of parable, makes one search for universal meanings which may not be there. She thought of her grandparents. Their love did not console her, was in fact a burden. She could never eat or wear enough to conciliate them with her way of life. Nor could she bring them any news that they would have wished to hear. She could not tell them what she had been doing, for in their eyes she had been doing nothing. The moral dilemmas of *Adolphe* would meet with total incomprehension, and she had the grace to spare them any self-important account of her success that afternoon, for it had been a success, she told herself. One always knew. Her landscape was as bare of imagery as *Adolphe* itself. She could not even tell Maurice, for his world was all of a piece; success in all one did was assumed without affectation. Besides, in his world, everyone was active and united. His mother sometimes came to his lectures, and was in the habit of driving off by herself to stay with friends in Scotland or Italy. People with houses.

It was a question of conditioning, thought Kitty Maule, as she hung up her skirt. I function well in one

51

sphere only, but all the others must be thought through, every day. Perhaps I will graft myself on to something native here, make a unity somehow. I can learn. I can understand. I can even criticize. What I cannot do is reconcile. I must work on that.

Into her dreams that night came the unbidden words, *'Mais quand on voit l'angoisse qui résulte de ces liens brisés* ... ', but she could not remember the rest.

F I V E

Kitty watched Maurice lower his spoon into his lemon pudding. She watched him until he had finished it, and as he helped himself to some more. He ate seriously, his eyes cast down.

'Is it all right?' she asked.

'Everything you do is all right,' he said, scraping his plate.

She blushed with pleasure. He had never spoken to her in this way before.

'No, I mean it,' he said. 'Redmile is astonishingly pleased with you. You seem to have done wonders with that group of his. He can't get over it.'

Kitty's pleasure dimmed a little. Professional success seemed to her of little importance compared with the risks she took in trying to please him. And anyway, teaching was something she could do on her own, with no reference to Maurice, and no need for his help, either. But with an inward sigh she took her cue from him; it was what he wanted, and he was here, after all. That was what mattered.

'They're very easy to get along with,' she said, piling their empty plates on to a tray. 'Larter you know, of course.' Everyone knew Larter, who had been cautioned for loitering outside the bicycle factory and who was capable of many embarrassing misdemeanours. 'Larter is, quite simply, brilliant. Mills will go back to his college and never be heard of again. But he's very nice. The one that worries me is Miss Fairchild. I can't seem to get any sense out of her. Shall we have our coffee by the window?'

Maurice took Kitty's cigarette out of her mouth, put it into his own, and passed it back to her.

'Jane Fairchild?' he asked. 'My mother thinks she's rather bright.'

'Your mother?' said Kitty in astonishment, receiving the cigarette back.

'She lives quite near us, in Gloucestershire. Her parents are friends of mine.'

'She's very beautiful,' said Kitty, digesting this news.

'Quite a pretty girl, yes.' He moved over to the sofa, stretched out his long legs, and crossing his hands behind his head, slid down until he was nearly horizontal. Kitty's eyes lingered lovingly on the crumpled cushions, displaced by his weight; they were always pristine when he was not here, and she hated them that way.

After a minute he turned to her and smiled. 'Where's that coffee?' he said.

Kitty made the coffee and served him. They drank in silence. After a minute, she asked him about his trip to France. 'More or less fixed,' he said, and patted the seat next to him for her to sit down. She waited to hear more but the subject appeared to be closed. He murmured something about the car needing to be taken into the garage the following week.

'And so you're off? When exactly?'

'Oh, three or four weeks' time. As soon as term is over. Actually, I might sneak off a bit early. And I'll stay there till the last minute. I'm not just inspecting these cathedrals, you know. They mean more to me than that.'

Kitty looked at him. His face, without its perpetual

smile was stern, sad. She had never seen him like this before.

'What is it, darling? Are you depressed?'

'No, my dear. I'm never depressed.'

Darling. My dear. Kitty registered this, their usual exchange of endearments. She registered it every time.

'Never depressed?' she asked, her voice a little false in her effort to keep her balance. 'I very much doubt if anyone else can say that. I'm depressed most of the time, I think.'

Maurice turned his head towards her and resumed his smile.

'Kitty,' he said. 'Kitty. You are absolutely without faith, aren't you?'

'Why, yes,' she said. 'How did you know?'

He smiled even more fully, at the look on her face. 'If you've got faith, you can always spot the ones without it. You, dearest Kitty, live in a world of unbelief. It makes you tense. I can't tell you how simple life is when you know that you are being looked after. How you can survive one blow after another.'

'Does God organize the blows?' asked Kitty, somewhat tartly.

'Who knows?'

'Then what exactly do you believe in?' asked Kitty.

Maurice took his arms from behind his neck and sat forward, elbows on his knees, staring at the floor.

'I believe in Providence,' he said.

Kitty was alarmed. He seemed strange this evening, locked up even more securely into his private world, allowing her no access. And she was aware, for the first time, that he was an adult, a man, not just a phenomenon, an unexpected visitor to her own life, but a human being whom experience had marked, who was beginning to show these marks, whose graceful body held its own inevitable diminutions.

She laid a hand on his arm. 'Maurice,' she said gently. 'You don't sound very happy when you talk of Providence. What is wrong?'

He took a long time answering. Then, locking his hands together between his knees, he stared at the floor, as if some image had suddenly materialized there, as if it held a fascination bordering on enchantment.

'What is wrong,' he said, 'is that I am without the one I love.'

Kitty sat very still. Her distress for him was almost as great as her distress for herself. The street lamp outside her window blurred for a moment; then, resolutely, she stared at it until it became clear again. 'That's all, folks,' cried an ebullient voice from the radio in Caroline's flat, followed by an injunction to the audience to take care of itself and be at the same place, same time, next week.

She turned her head to look at him.

'Won't you tell me about it?' she asked, and her voice was just the same as it always was.

He still sat staring at the floor, his hands knotted, his expression bleak. After a long pause he turned to her and looked at her as if she were a stranger. When he began to speak, it was as if his voice were coming from a long distance, from far back in his skull, as if it were travelling over territories of experience which Kitty had never even glimpsed.

'Tell?' he said. 'There's nothing to tell.'

'Oh, Maurice,' said Kitty sadly. 'Don't you trust me?'

He smiled at her briefly, then returned his gaze to the floor.

'No, really,' he said. 'There's nothing to tell. I never talk about it. I was in love with this girl and we were looking forward to getting married but she discovered that she had a vocation. She's working with Mother Teresa in Calcutta. That's all.'

'What was her name?' asked Kitty.

56

'Lucy. She was called Lucy. I've known her all my life. We always loved each other. Our parents were neighbours.' He broke off, but Kitty sensed that he was now ready to talk.

'Shall I make some more coffee?' she asked.

'Yes, why not?'

He followed her into the kitchen, as if unwilling to be left alone. His presence, and the words she had just heard, disturbed her, and she spilled a little water from the kettle. Picking up a dishcloth, he wiped the drops from the floor.

'You're as bad as Lucy,' he said. 'She was the most untidy creature I have ever met.'

'Did you love her very much?' said Kitty, willing her hands to remain still.

'Yes, of course. Enough to last me for the rest of my life. Shall I take that tray?'

They sat down again, silent. A burst of urgent music from the next flat signified a change of programme. Then Maurice sighed.

'I know that she prays for me,' he said. 'As I pray for her. I know that we shall never be closer than we are now.' He sighed again. 'I am so bored without her to talk to,' he said. 'We always shared everything. I have no one to talk to now.'

This time she took him in her arms and held him, and as they sat together in the darkening room she felt her whole heart dissolving in sadness and wonder.

It was Maurice who disengaged himself, and to her surprise he recovered quite quickly. His smile, vague, pleasant, prohibitive of deeper enquiries, was back in place. He drank his cold coffee and held out his cup for more. Kitty, aware that they were passing a momentous evening, yet fearful of all that she had heard, and uncertain how they could proceed after this, went into the kitchen, her hands unusually agitated. He should have told me this before, she thought. I would have understood all that. But I lacked the information. Quite simply, I lacked the information.

Returning to the sofa, and to Maurice, with more, unwanted, coffee, she said, 'And are you still on God's side?' She was genuinely curious.

His smile intensified, became ineffable. 'Don't you see? God is on *my* side. He gave me years of happiness and love that can never disappear. I regard myself as married. It is as simple as that.'

Oh, Maurice, thought Kitty. I shall never know what you feel. The intensity. The purity. I simply want to live with someone so that I can begin my life. I want you, in fact. And you want nobody.

'Maurice,' she said, taking his hand. 'I do understand. And please, please, trust me. I am your friend.'

He kissed her hand. 'Of course, I trust you. Dear Kitty.'

They both realized that this was the moment at which he should leave, that there could be no further exchange that night. Yet she had never wanted so much for him to stay.

'Maurice,' she said, as he searched in his pocket for his car keys. 'When did all this happen?'

'Three years ago,' he replied, then, having found his keys, he kissed her lightly on the cheek and was gone.

Three years ago Marie-Thérèse had died, quickly, quietly, without benefit of clergy, without assurance of eternal comfort, her hands trailing among the walnut shells. They never spoke of her at home, and indeed Kitty herself thought little about the matter. She was aware that the world had grown colder since Marie-Thérèse's death, that a particular quick artless voice would no longer question her, that a certain shyness and propriety had vanished from her own life, leaving behind something wary, fearful, disbelieving. This corroding residue was apt to interfere with her more generous impulses, and she had to struggle these days to trust her earlier, more primitive assumptions of safety. It was a feeling she only managed to recover among her books. And it had been revealed to her this evening, this momentous evening, that there was a safety beyond anything she had ever known, that the love of one person for another can confer such a charmed life that even the memory of it bestows immunity. She herself was not immune. And if she had one wish, it was to know that immunity, to be loved in such a way that even when parted from the other she would never be alone. She wondered if there were anything in her life, in herself, that could make her lovable in that way, and realized that there was nothing, not even a basis for comparison. Perhaps it was because she lacked faith, as Maurice said, that she was tense, that she could not take life more easily, that she could not take him for granted. For surely, they were dearest friends? Surely, he would not talk as he had talked tonight to anyone else?

But I want more, she thought, blowing her nose resolutely. I do not want to be trustworthy, and safe, and discreet. I do not want to be the one who understands and sympathizes and soothes. I do not want to be reliable, I do not want to do wonders with Professor Redmile's group, I do not even care what happens to Larter. I do not want to be good at pleasing everybody. I do not even want to be such a good cook, she thought, turning the tap with full force on to a bowl rusted with the stains of her fresh tomato soup. I want to be totally unreasonable, totally unfair, very demanding, and very beautiful. I want to be part of a real family. I want my father to be there and to shoot things. I do not want my grandmother to tell me what to wear. I want to wear jeans and old sweaters belonging to my brother whom of course I do not have. I do not want to spend my life in this rotten little flat. I want wedding presents. I want to be half of a recognized couple. I want a future away from this place. I want Maurice.

'Caroline,' she said, striding out of her front door, her cheeks scarlet with emotion. 'Will you please turn your radio down? I can hear every word of the shipping forecast *and* I've got the tap running.'

Caroline's door opened, to reveal Caroline in her usual *poule de luxe* outfit of pale blue and purple flowered chiffon dressing gown with, yes, marabout at the throat, and very high-heeled mules. Her toenails were painted an iridescent damson colour. Her orange hair was shining, her face fully made-up, as if she were expecting a visitor. If she was, he never came. He had gone long ago, that husband whom she reviled so constantly. Kitty sometimes regretted the impulse that had made them into the semblance of friends. Caroline had called when Kitty had first moved in, and Kitty had been drawn to her as a really well-dressed woman, something she rarely came across in her line of work. They had spent a few evenings together comparing notes on clothes, until Kitty realized, with a feeling of shame, that Caroline was intensely boring. Or perhaps, she thought scrupulously, she was just intensely bored. Caroline lived on her alimony and consulted fortune tellers to see when her luck would change. Caroline spent most of her days, impeccably groomed, wandering around Harrods. Very little seemed to happen to Caroline although she had many stories to tell of her life before she had been abandoned: the parties, the cruises, the weekends at important houses. 'Why did I marry him?' she would ask soulfully. Why did he leave you, wondered Kitty, but was too polite to ask. She rather dreaded Caroline's reminiscences these days and tended to avoid her. She had once seen her coming down Old Church Street, presumably returning from a day at

Harrods, and had noted that there was a ladder in her tights and that she was carrying an umbrella and two rather crumpled plastic bags, the very image, Kitty thought, of a woman slipping down from her own high standards. She had felt a shiver of apprehension, and at the moment considered herself the more fortunate of the two. For she had Maurice.

'What is it, Kitty?' asked Caroline in genuine surprise. 'You sound really upset. Didn't you have a nice evening?'

It had been impossible to keep the sight of Maurice hurtling up the stairs from Caroline, and that was another reason for Kitty to want to avoid her: Caroline was avid for information, and Kitty had no information to give.

'Come in,' said Caroline, 'I've just made a cup of tea.' She was desperately lonely.

At that moment Kitty wanted nothing more than a cup of tea. She wanted it with a passion that she had not felt for food or drink for a very long time. Wiping her hands on her apron, and aware that she must look a mess, she followed Caroline into her flat.

'Marvellous tea,' she acknowledged. 'But really, Caroline, the noise is too much. And you know you don't really listen.'

'Oh, darling, I keep it on for company. You know what it's like here in the evenings. Dead. I might as well be ninety. When I think ... '

'All the same,' said Kitty, holding out her cup for more and forestalling the usual recital, 'it is a bit much. Oh, I realize you're lonely. Perhaps if you got a job?' They had had this conversation before.

'I'd still be alone in the evenings,' said Caroline. This was unanswerable.

'How was your boyfriend?' asked Caroline after a pause.

'Oh, fine, fine.'

'You're upset, Kitty. Oh, men. You don't have to tell *me*.'

You wouldn't understand if I did, thought Kitty. No one would. Maurice's story now appeared to her as something she could never tell a living soul. It was, after all, a secret.

'Tell you what, darling,' said Caroline. 'Why don't you come with me to this marvellous clairvoyant I've just discovered? No really, Kitty, she's fantastic. I know you don't believe in them, but this one is different. She told me all about Paul and how life was so stagnant at the moment, and how I was going to make a new life abroad, and meet a man whose name begins with J. In the entertainment business. Well, that's not really my line, you know. I'm used to rather better than that. Did I ever tell you about the time we chartered a yacht off Saint-Tropez?'

She had. Many times.

But a thought was forming in Kitty's mind. Supposing she went to this clairvoyant, made a firm declaration of her scepticism, and then waited to hear what she said? She needed a message, desperately. For Maurice had not said when he would see her again. And soon he would be off to the cathedrals of France.

'Where is she?' she enquired.

'My dear, she's two minutes from here, just next door to the antique market. And it's only ten pounds. And she's marvellous. She told me all about the lease running out.' (This was another frequent topic of conversation.) 'And she told me I was looking for another flat but that I didn't need to bother because I was going to meet this man beginning with J. In the entertainment business.'

'All right,' said Kitty grimly. 'I'll come with you.'

Caroline's face lit up. She was easily pleased and just as easily disappointed.

62

'We'll go next week,' she promised. 'You'll see. Everything will come out right.'

'I hope so,' said Kitty. The sudden silence informed her that the radio had gone off the air for the night. It must be quite late. She did not have the heart to speak to Caroline again about the noise. She knew it would make no difference anyway.

Trudging back across the landing to her own flat, she was aware that she was very tired. The evening now appeared to her in retrospect as completely unreal. Had she really heard what she had heard? Could she, she thought disgustedly, compare her visit to a fortune teller with Maurice's profound convictions? And yet she was disturbed, moved, but moved for herself as well. I must do something, she thought. We cannot go on as we are. If we do I cannot bear it.

As she lay in bed it occurred to her to turn to Marie-Thérèse's Bible and to seek out the passage that had originally comforted her. But she felt unworthy, not a believer. Maurice had talked about Providence. She was a determinist, herself. But she would give it a try, she thought wearily. Are You there she wondered, in the silence. And if so, will You let me hear from You?

S I X

For the visit to the clairvoyant Caroline wore violet trousers, a blue silk shirt, and several chains round her neck. Dressing the part, thought Kitty, watching her twine a blue trailing scarf round her hair. And she's not even coming in.

'Isn't this fun, Kitty?' enthused Caroline, discarding the blue scarf for a green one, and then discarding that. Kitty sank resignedly into a chair.

Her mood was uneasy. Part of her was deeply ashamed of what she was doing. Another part of her was aware that this line of enquiry might easily become an addiction, that if she heard good news she would go back to hear more, and that if she heard bad news she would go back to see when her luck would change. And she would not know, actually know as she had been taught to know, anything at all. She was intellectually, as well as morally, uneasy. But it was all fixed now; Caroline had made the appointment, although they had had to wait for nearly two weeks, and had given a false name, for some reason. This too was further cause for shame.

There were additional rumours of unease. On the telephone, the previous evening, Louise's breathing had sounded more laboured than usual, and she had given the telephone back to Vadim to finish the conversation.

'What is the matter?' Kitty had asked him. She was a little tired, he had said: the weather was so unseasonably warm. She has her bad days. But nothing to worry about. He sounded sad, out of character. 'Papa,' said Kitty, 'call the doctor.' No, no, my darling, everything was all right. He had bought artichokes as a treat. Louisette loved artichokes. And there was a good programme on television. She would be better tomorrow, have no fear. Kitty had not had the heart to tell him that Pauline Bentley had invited her home for the weekend. She would cancel it if necessary.

There was also the matter of her lecture on the Romantic Tradition, timed for the fourth week of the summer term. She had done no preliminary work for this, yet she was aware that it was something of a test. If she acquitted herself well, it might lead to a proper appointment. As it was, she was a sort of guest in the department, being paid for the seminars she gave, but regarded as a more or less permanent researcher. But if her lecture were to be a success, she could regard her investigation, her apprenticeship, as finished.

Her seminar the previous week had not gone as smoothly as she had hoped. Miss Fairchild being inexplicably absent, Larter and Mills had argued without restraint, both revealing rather more bad temper than was proper to the occasion. They were tired; it was getting near the end of term, and they had grown pale on cheap food and not enough fresh air. Kitty had decided to cut the afternoon short, for it would not get better, and had called a final class for the following week. This had not been a popular suggestion, and later that day Redmile had asked her how she was getting on. 'Very well,' she had said, smiling at him. 'We are all looking forward to your lecture, Miss Maule.' This was patently false, so she went on smiling at him. 'Great stuff. Great stuff.' He always said this. Then his eyes lit up as his secretary approached with a file. 'Have you got the latest estimates, Jennifer? Well, I mustn't keep you, Miss Maule. And I think Jennifer has something to show me. The New Building, you know.' And he was gone.

Kitty felt a sort of irritated langour, very different from her usual state of calm if timid determination. Although she looked on Caroline's activities sternly, she wondered with genuine humility if she could ever be such a woman, delighting in her own appearance, devoting much time and effort to embellishing it, regarding her small outing as a genuine point of reference in the day, fascinated by her ultimate fate and waiting for others to bring it about. Kitty had frequently felt that she lacked some essential feminine quality, that this resided in the folklore passed on by women who possessed a knowledge that she was forced to supplement by reading books. She had sometimes, but with a curious sense of secrecy, scanned the advice columns in the magazines she bought for Louise, even studied the horoscopes. She knew that she had chosen a more severe path of ascertainable information, but she was lured by the stratagems, the reassurances, the promises of that odd sub-consciousness shared greedily by, she supposed, women with a surer touch than herself. There must be ways of getting what she wanted, but she did not know what they were. This visit to the clairvoyant held out the dangerous attraction of such a hidden way, just as Caroline, with her confident and gratuitous self-adornment, represented another mode of being. As if Caroline, regarding herself as a prize, were simply waiting for someone to come and claim her. Whereas Kitty usually felt that she was the one who had to prove her worth, her desirability, her merit, her right. As if she lived in a world where moral imperatives obtained. She felt that she was serving an apprenticeship in more ways than one, and that, by analogy, she had to work hard on all fronts. She longed to join that more confident majority that made assumptions, that imposed a sense of superiority whether it had any basis in fact or not. She had been amused but also genuinely impressed by a small incident in the newspaper shop a few days previously. The girl behind the counter, a stringy and exhausted blonde, was selling a packet of cigarettes to a handsome young labourer from a nearby building site. The man had held out a ten-pound note. 'Oh Christ,' said the girl, 'haven't you got anything smaller? I'll have to go next door for some change.' 'So what?' he grinned. 'Aren't I worth it?' 'Dunno,' said the girl, without a change of expression. 'Haven't tried you yet, have I?' They were both delighted with this exchange. Kitty had joined in the laughter but had felt prim, knowing that she could never achieve such ease of manner, knowing also that on occasions it might be appropriate.

They were passing this same shop on their way to the clairvoyant. Caroline undulated like a siren, clutching her bag, her scarves, touching her chains, her feet slipping about in ridiculously fragile sandals. From time to time she had to steady herself by hanging on to Kitty who assumed a martyr-like pose of rigid stillness until all the necessary adjustments had been made and they could start off again. She wondered how Caroline ever managed to get to Harrods on her own. She also knew that Caroline could walk as easily as anyone else, and was using her as a convenient foil in the absence of a man. She was thankful that no public transport was needed, for Caroline would expect her to organize their journey, pay their fares, if there were a bus coming, or to step into the road and summon a taxi if there were none. Kitty mused on this. She supposed that it was the equivalent of negative capability, something she had always attributed to certain aspects of behaviour rather than to modes of perception.

They turned down a small alley and stopped outside a mean front door painted bottle green. As Caroline rang the bell a cat, startled, plunged off the windowsill, knocking over two milk bottles. While Kitty was picking these up and restoring them to their rightful place by the step, the door opened and a neat-looking elderly woman – Madame Eva, Kitty thought to herself with a thrill of shame – appeared. 'Hello, my darling,' she said to Caroline. 'Brought your friend, have you?' Caroline made the introductions as if she were at a rather smart party. 'Madame Eva,' she said, taking the woman's hand. 'I want you to meet my friend, Miss Mortimer.' Kitty took a deep breath. She supposed that having an abortion was something like this. 'How do you do?' she heard herself saying. 'I shan't keep you long. By the way, my name is Maule. Kitty Maule.' She was aware of some asperity in her manner, and took another deep breath. 'I'll see you at home later, Caroline.' Caroline's face fell. Madame Eva turned a mild but shrewd glance in her direction. 'Why don't you wait next door, in the café?' she said. 'Then you can go home together.' Anything to get this over, thought Kitty. I should never have come. I should have stayed at home with *Adolphe* and the Romantic Tradition. That is where I belong. But she had ventured so far outside her role that she could do nothing but follow the woman into the house, while Caroline waved encouragingly and turned her tottering footsteps towards the antique market. Kitty knew that the moment she was out of sight she would resume her normal brisk tread. As indeed she did.

Madame Eva's consulting room was small, dark, dingy, indeterminate and oddly comfortable. It represented perhaps the ultimate mess or primal ooze from which vatic female pronouncements would appropriately emerge. Dirty cushions softened the shapes of a couple of sagging armchairs, two of them placed in close proximity. A radio was playing very softly, a cat was asleep under a table, and on another table lay the remains of a frugal lunch. Madame Eva herself looked like the headmistress of a decent primary school. She was reassuringly plump, neatly groomed, and spotlessly clean; indeed she was rather attractively dressed in a loose flowered smock, which reinforced the infants' school image, with her spectacles hanging on a chain round her neck. She moved slowly and with great deliberation, switching off the radio, getting rid of the cat, settling herself in one armchair while motioning Kitty to the other. Reaching into a leatherette shopping bag by the side of her chair she brought out a Thermos flask and a mug and poured herself a quantity of orange tea. While she sipped this, she studied Kitty's face. Kitty forced herself to look steadily back. This was an initiation ten times worse than her lecture would be. Thank God Maurice will never know about this, she thought. The woman smiled. 'Thinking of your boyfriend?' she said.

Because the room was so dark, Kitty was aware of the brightness and stillness of the afternoon. Sunlight glinted off the rim of the woman's spectacles, and the warmth brought a comfortable frowsty odour out of the cushions. She did not know how long she had been there, while Madame Eva sipped her tea, and did not much care. She felt oddly safe, for this was a secret place. A total silence enveloped her, a silence ultimately broken only by the small cawing noise of the Thermos flask being screwed up. This was set aside on the table, ready for further libations. Then the hand descended again into the leatherette bag and produced a small crystal ball.

Madame Eva leaned over Kitty's cupped hands. 'I see a man,' she said. Her voice was not up to the standard of her appearance, held indeed the faint whine of the professional gipsy. Kitty's heart began to beat rather hard. With alarm and surprise she felt herself surrendering to the occasion. 'A man,' repeated Madame Eva. 'Very tall. Nice looking. Clever. You met him through your work.' Kitty nodded. The woman breathed heavily. 'Now I'm getting a relative. Elderly lady. Bit of trouble there. But not yet. In the future. Be prepared. I see a foreign city.' She stopped abruptly and wiped a little moisture from the sides of her mouth. 'Doesn't half take it out of you, this work,' she said to Kitty. 'Sometimes in the evenings I can't even do me hair, I'm so tired.' Her hair, a heavily lacquered pyramid the colour of dirty brass, evidently took some doing. She bent over Kitty's hands again. 'I see a tall building. Like a church. I see you going in. Might be a wedding. Don't think so. Might be. I can't see. Hang on, darling, I'll have a drop more tea.'

The Thermos flask was unscrewed once more. Cathedrals of France, thought Kitty, it can only mean that. The heat in the room became more intense, generated apparently by the efforts of the woman to put her thoughts into words. For although Kitty was impressed by her insights, she was distracted by Madame Eva's evident inarticulacy. As a teacher she found herself rephrasing the information, and felt it growing richer as she did so.

'You're very clever,' said the fortune teller. 'There's a lot of success ahead. You've no need to worry about money. You'll be well looked after. Even more in the future.' Kitty was not interested in this information, for she possessed it already. But she supposed it was just this that people came to hear.

The woman turned the crystal ball in Kitty's palms. 'I keep getting this big building. And this foreign city.' She looked at Kitty over the tops of her glasses. 'Were you thinking of going abroad?' Kitty found herself nodding, appalled and enthralled at the prospects opening in front of her. 'That's it, then,' said Madame Eva. 'You're going away somewhere.' She breathed heavily again. 'I see a lady. Your mother? Has she passed?' Kitty looked at her uncomprehendingly. 'Mother,' repeated the woman. 'Has she passed on?' Kitty nodded again, her throat thickening. This surprised her, for she had never wept for her mother, had never dared to. Did not even dare to think of Marie-Thérèse as her mother. The conjunction of the person and the concept would have moved her in a way she could not afford to imagine. 'Mother's watching,' said Madame Eva. Tears spilled over from Kitty's eyes. 'All right, darling,' said Madame Eva. 'Mother's watching.'

She sat back with a sigh and poured out the last dregs of tea from her flask. 'Was there anything you wanted to ask me, dear?'

'Tell me about the man,' said Kitty, lost to all sense of propriety.

Madame Eva sighed again and bent once more over the crystal ball. 'I think he loves you,' she said. 'But it's not clear. Someone's holding him back. Is he married?'

Kitty shook her head, unable to speak.

'He's connected to someone,' said the medium. 'A girl.' She seemed suddenly abstracted. 'Very clever,' she said vaguely. 'Ends badly.' This meant nothing to Kitty but echoed her own feelings about the Lucy story. 'He's clever, and all,' said the woman with a sudden return of sharpness. 'Try your luck, dear. Try your luck abroad.'

Kitty handed over ten pounds in a daze of gratitude. She crept out into the sun-struck alley on shaking legs, her course of action at last clear to her. Without noticing, she found herself wandering into the antique market, where a blaze of colour indicated Caroline, perched on a stool, with two cups of tea waiting. All this tea, thought Kitty, but drank it gratefully. Her hands,

71

she was not surprised to note, were trembling. I must grow up, she thought. I must stop being so humble. I can make decisions and initiate actions like anyone else. I am not stupid. I am not poor. If I want to do something I do not have to wait for permission. I am old enough to make up my own mind. My mother was a widow at eighteen. My father was a corpse at twenty-one. I am wasting time. I shall waste no more.

'Well?' said Caroline.

'She's good,' said Kitty soberly, although she could no longer remember precisely what she had been told. She remembered the little room, and the sunlight glinting off the spectacles, and the smell of the cushions, and the improbably coiffed hair bending over the crystal ball in front of her. She had gathered no information but some kind of shift in her consciousness had taken place.

She found it difficult to tell Caroline, who of course had to be told, what she herself had heard. She remembered with a stab of alarm what Madame Eva had said about an elderly relative, and resolved to go and see her grandparents that evening and not to wait until the weekend. She felt tired and sad and somehow older.

'But what about your boyfriend?' Caroline persisted. This was what it was all about, in her opinion. This was the point of visiting Madame Eva in the first place.

There was an odd obscurity surrounding what Madame Eva had said about Maurice. She had grasped the essentials of his situation, of the circumstances of their meeting; she had seen Lucy. She had mentioned love. She had seen his 'marriage', still, apparently, in operation. She had seen them abroad. A church. A large church. A cathedral, in fact.

'She didn't say much,' Kitty told Caroline, to the latter's evident disappointment.

Kitty felt a sudden warmth for Caroline, who had

taken the trouble to dress up simply in order to sit in the malodorous antique market, when she could have been putting in an afternoon at Harrods. But as Caroline wound and unwound her scarf, putting the final touches to her appearance for the short journey home, Kitty knew that she could not tolerate playing the supporting role any longer.

'I'll have to leave you here,' she said. 'I want to go over and see my grandmother. If I go now, I can just beat the rush hour.' She marvelled at her own ruthlessness, and as Caroline's expression darkened – for she was upset, she had not heard what she wanted to hear – Kitty leaned forward and kissed her, a thing she had never done before, and turned resolutely out into the sunny street, and, after a minute, was on a bus to Victoria.

During the short but tedious journey to her grandparents' house, Kitty Maule reflected on her present situation. Now that the emotion was ebbing away (but leaving her very tired), she thought pityingly of her former passivity, her illusion that time would sort out the present, that she need only wait, feeding on the sort of hope represented by a random passage from her mother's Bible. But I must act, she thought. I am a total bore as I am. A nonentity. Not even a pawn in the game. She began to review her clothes, mentally consigning those which were safe and neutral and represented her grandmother's outdated notions of classic good taste to the back of her cupboard. All around her in the train were girls not much younger than herself in trousers and pullovers, their hair long and unkempt and naturally untidy, their faces bare of artifice. Kitty in fact thought they might look better with a little make-up, with a little more effort. But I may be wrong, she said to herself. I may be too static, too formal.

She put her key in the lock of her grandparents'

house, and heard voices raised in enquiry, in French. Then the television was turned off. An exquisite aromatic smell drifted out from under the door of their living room. As she opened it, she met Papa's alarmed face on the other side.

'What is it, Thérèse?' he said. 'Are you ill, my darling?'

She gave him the bunch of narcissus she had bought at the florist's next to the station. She kissed him. 'I just felt like seeing you,' she said. His face flooded with his great final-curtain smile.

Kitty saw them both, with napkins tied round their necks, butter smeared on their chins, the leaves of artichokes discarded on an extra plate between the two of them. They had been eating in front of the television, for they no longer bothered much with the formalities of living. Louise, Kitty noted with relief, did not look particularly ill. She did not look particularly well, either. She had become enormously stout, and tended to wear the same dusty black dress all the time, a small crocheted triangular shawl, like that of a concierge, around her shoulders. Louise noted her glance. She smiled, but her eyes narrowed slightly.

'Eh, oui,' she conceded. 'Nous dinons en grande toilette, comme d'habitude.'

After which they all laughed. Kitty laughed in gratitude, for her grandmother was undiminished. Madame Eva had said there was no need to worry yet. And indeed there was no time. She decided to postpone Pauline Bentley's invitation to the following weekend; she would be the daughter at home again, once more. Perhaps for not much longer, she thought.

Together they watched a television programme about baby seals. The heartfelt commentary, destined to awake their compassion, fell on deaf ears, for Louise thought that sealskin made a marvellous coat for the

74

older woman, and Vadim and Kitty were not listening anyway.

When she left them, after a cup of tisane, it was dark, but she was aware that the year was opening up, that the blue dusk was not so impenetrable as it had been. Easter, which was late, would soon be here. A faint keen sharpness, rather than a smell, was in the air, from uncurling privet buds. On an impulse, she took the one taxi outside the station and rode all the way back to Old Church Street. At home, Caroline's radio was too loud, as usual, but she could afford to ignore that now. Without taking off her coat, she went to the telephone and dialled Maurice's number. There was no answer. She wandered into the kitchen and ate an apple, then into her bedroom. She was oddly nervous, her earlier resolution faltering now that she was back in familiar surroundings. She tried Maurice's number again. Still no answer. She took a bath, ate another apple, got into bed and tried to read. Shortly after eleven, she telephoned again. This time he answered immediately.

'Maurice,' she said. 'Am I disturbing you? It's Kitty, by the way.'

'I know it's Kitty,' he said mildly. 'What can I do for you?'

She took a deep breath.

'I've decided to go to Paris to work on my lecture a bit. There are one or two things I need to look up. Can we meet there?'

He laughed. 'That might be a bit difficult, my dear. I'm driving around, as you know. When will you be there?'

'I'm not sure,' said Kitty. 'But it seems so silly, our being practically in the same place and not meeting.' She was aware that she was pleading and took hold of herself.

'If you're going to do Saint-Denis, you'll have to come

through Paris. Although,' she added scrupulously, 'Saint-Denis is an abbey church, not a cathedral.'

'You're right,' he pondered. 'But I do love all those tombs.' There was a silence. 'Why not?' he said. 'I could pick you up on my way back. Where will you be?'

'At the Hotel West End,' she said. 'Just off the Avenue Montaigne.' She had already decided this in the taxi.

He laughed. 'Ridiculous Kitty. But it would be nice. I'll give you a call there at the end of the month, then.' And he rang off.

Kitty Maule slept badly that night. But the following morning she woke up with renewed energy and began to make further plans.

SEVEN

Kitty, who had become rather thin, looked at her pale face in the glass and decided after all to accept Pauline Bentley's invitation for the weekend, hoping that she might return to London looking rosy and refreshed. The whole point of this was to appear in a good light when she got to Paris. She did not know Pauline Bentley well but they enjoyed the unsentimental abstracted comradeship of those who understand each other's work. Pauline Bentley lived with her mother in a cottage in Gloucestershire, and to Kitty Gloucestershire was hallowed ground. I might as well familiarize myself with the layout, she thought, as if Gloucestershire were a piece of research.

As indeed it seemed to be. For as she sat in the train, and the mild country opened out on either side of her, she searched herself in vain for a response to nature that would do honour to one whose subject was the Romantic Tradition, and found none. But maybe this is the wrong terrain, she thought. Romantic heroes always seem to be wandering among ruins or cataracts or mountains; the weather is stormy or it is nightfall; they have been thinking about immortality or going mad; they wear dishevelled frock-coats and have one foot braced against a rock; and, as is well known, they think it better to travel hopefully than to arrive. Nature imposes such obligations upon them to understand it or rather her. Nature, the great female corollary to God, is as uncomprehending and as incomprehensible as her masculine analogue. This Kitty understood. She also understood the need to get closer to both, to scan them for a meaning or for an answer. If possible for an answer. But any response was usually one of their own fabrication and so that argument was circular. On the whole, she thought, looking out gravely on to the sunlit fields, there is less obfuscation when nature is out of the way. The author of *Adolphe* is entirely correct when he sets his story *'dans la petite ville de D——'*. I hadn't realized how very clever the book was. Everything in it is accurate and pitiless, and contained in the author's own reflections. There are no objective correlatives. There are no answers. And there are no excuses, either.

Pauline Bentley was waiting at the small station, dressed in her usual tweed suit, a King Charles spaniel seated mournfully at her feet. At the sight of Pauline, a thin clever woman, Kitty was once again reminded of what awaited her if her life failed to change. Pauline was a gifted and honourable teacher but she was admired rather than liked, for years of hiding her feelings had made her sarcastic, unsentimental, in a way that was good for departmental efficiency but bad for students looking for the sort of glamorous governess figure they were prepared to tolerate in a female tutor. Pauline lived with her widowed mother, who was nearly blind; she drove from the university every night to this small place, with the shopping in the back of the car. When she got home, she would switch on the lights, for it made no difference to her mother whether she sat in the dark or not, put a match to the fire, and cook the dinner. Her mother liked to hear all the news. She had been a distinguished don herself, and prided herself on keeping in touch. She found her daughter praiseworthy but unambitious, and urged her constantly to publish more. Washing up in the chilly kitchen, Pauline would shift from one aching foot to the other and think only of her electric blanket and the World Service of the B.B.C. which would keep her company through her increasingly sleepless nights. She was glad that Kitty had come down to take some of the weight off her shoulders.

'We might as well have a cup of coffee here,' said Pauline, rousing the dog. 'Then all I have to do is the lunch when we get home. I hope you don't mind ham and salad. Mother is so looking forward to meeting you,' she added, striding on ahead.

The dog was very old, and did not seem particularly viable. Kitty looked on it with some disfavour, but it had attached itself to her unquestioningly, apparently unaware of her feelings. Its sleeping weight was unpleasantly warm against her leg under the table in the café, which was also very warm, and extremely full. Disconsolate families ate baked beans on toast and wrapped handkerchiefs around the stinging handles of metal teapots, for this was tourist country, Kitty realized, and the season was beginning. The two waitresses, middle-aged women, called haplessly to one another and forgot orders which they were too harassed to write down. The little space between the tables was clogged by shopping baskets, a push chair, and, of course, the dog. Even I could run this place better, thought Kitty, who was not impressed. She had her grandmother's contempt for amateurishness. To Pauline it was a useful place to fill in time until the pub opened. She rarely noticed what she ate or drank, in any case.

'How's the lecture going?' she asked Kitty. And she is the only person who really wants to know, thought Kitty. And I haven't given it much thought.

'I haven't given it much thought,' she answered. 'I shan't be able to until the term is over. I've had to do rather more teaching than I bargained for.'

'Let's see,' said Pauline. 'You've got Larter, haven't you? Yes, he takes a bit of keeping up with. He takes up a lot of time too.'

'It's not a bad group,' said Kitty. 'Although last week it wasn't much of a group. Miss Fairchild didn't turn up. I'd better find out if she's ill, I suppose.'

'Jane? Oh, she's all right. I saw her in the village before I picked you up.'

'Does she live here?' asked Kitty in some surprise.

'My dear, the Fairchilds practically own the place.'

'And,' said Kitty with studied calm, 'Maurice Bishop is around here somewhere, isn't he?'

'Yes,' said Pauline, heaving a large wristwatch into sight and kicking the dog awake. 'A bit further out. We've just got time for a quick gin before Mother starts to worry.'

Kitty, who was disappointed at hearing so little, but was determined not to ask for details, followed Pauline into the pub, as did half the inhabitants of the café. I shall learn nothing, she thought. And at this rate I shall not get much fresh air either.

After three-quarters of an hour in the pub, they transferred themselves to Pauline's small car, which immediately filled up with the smell of dog. They travelled silently for about six miles, and then stopped abruptly by the telephone box opposite the row of four cottages that composed Pauline's village. Kitty felt a pang of pain for her. She comes here every night, even in the darkest winter, she said to herself. There is no one for her to talk to. She has to make arrangements for people to come in and see to her mother during the day. And when her mother dies, what will she do? Probably go on living in the same place, even lonelier. And she knows all this. She is too clever not to know. She is what is called a liberated woman, thought Kitty. The kind

80

envied by captive housewives. She felt an urgent need to put her own life into some sort of order, to ensure that she did not turn out like Caroline or like Pauline, the one so stupid, the other so intelligent, and both so bereft. She saw her two friends, who would have nothing to say to each other if they should ever meet, as casualties of the same conflict, as losers in the war in which Providence was deemed to play so large a part, and to determine the outcome, for some, not for others.

'I hope you're not going to be bored,' Pauline's voice broke in at this point. 'Mother likes me to spend as much time as possible with her at the weekends. But that leaves you quite free. You could be an angel and take the dog out. If he can keep awake, that is. He gets no exercise at all.'

Kitty breathed conscientiously as she got out of the car, as people will when they think it is going to do them good. Pauline, who was aware of the existence of the nuclear power plant twenty-five hazy miles distant, smiled wryly to herself but said nothing. Years of living with her mother had made her adept at keeping bad news to herself.

But Mrs Bentley and Kitty were delighted with each other. In a cool low-ceilinged little room, its windows obscured by fleshy green plants in brass pots, Kitty sat on a stool beside a wing chair, while Pauline retired to the kitchen and got on with the lunch. Mrs Bentley, in the chair, put out a large shaking liver-spotted hand, and Kitty took it and held it for a moment between both of her own. She noted the bony but still active frame, the man's handkerchief protruding from the pocket of the cardigan, the thin white hair following the shape of the large skull, the long narrow feet passive in childish sandals.

'Now, my dear,' said Mrs Bentley, in her rather carrying lecturer's voice. 'You must tell me who you are and what you are, for I can't see a thing for myself you know.'

'I am called Kitty,' said Kitty, 'although my name is Thérèse. I work with Pauline in ... '

'Why are you called Kitty if your name is Thérèse?' asked Mrs Bentley with great interest. And Kitty, who did not normally talk about such matters, found herself telling Mrs Bentley about her grandparents and her mother and father; it was not much of a story but it pleased Mrs Bentley, who got rather tired of Radio Three, placed conveniently near her chair. Kitty's story was like one of the Edwardian novels she could no longer read. When Pauline came back with the tray and started arranging plates on a small table which she moved close to her mother's chair, Kitty was describing her mother's wedding dress, now shrouded in tissue paper, but still hanging in her grandparents' flat, and the small satin shoes that went with it.

'But that is charming!' cried Mrs Bentley. 'And do you speak French at home? That must give you a head start with your work.'

Pauline smiled faintly as she moved a plate, on which the food was cut into small pieces, and touched her mother's wrist to it. Mrs Bentley took a fork in her shaking hand, and they began their lunch.

'I don't get out now,' said Mrs Bentley in a matter of fact voice. 'Except when Pauline takes me in the car and then I feel a little dizzy, not being able to see.'

'My grandmother never goes out,' said Kitty, retrieving a slice of tomato which was slowly descending the rugged surface of Mrs Bentley's cardigan.

'I wish we could meet. Old women have such a lot to talk about, even if they don't know each other. And the two of us with only one daughter.'

For a moment they all contemplated this possibility. Then they recognized it as an impossibility, and dis-

82

carded it. Pauline glanced swiftly at Kitty, who was mopping up Mrs Bentley's spilled glass of water with her handkerchief. When she saw that Kitty's face was calm and unembarrassed, she relaxed. Kitty, for her part, was not unused to the petty squalors of old age, and did not think about them. She worried far more about being her own age and not making the most of it.

They had a cup of coffee; Mrs Bentley took a battered tin and a packet of cigarette papers out of the pocket of her cardigan and began to roll a cigarette between large trembling fingers. When ignited, it burned like a flare for a second or two and then went out.

'Will you have one of mine, Mrs Bentley?' asked Kitty.

'No thank you, my dear, I really just like messing about with my tin. Habit, really. It was my husband's, you see. And anyway, I usually have my rest about now. Pauline can show you the garden. But I want so much to hear about your work – perhaps after tea you will tell me about your lecture. I have kept in touch, you know. After all, my generation was the first to read *The Romantic Agony*. My husband and I called on Professor Praz in Rome when we were on our wedding journey.' She leaned back in her chair, groped on the top of the radio for a large green silk handkerchief, and draped it over her face. Within seconds she was asleep. Pauline lifted a corner of the handkerchief, lowered it gently, and motioned Kitty to follow her into the kitchen.

'You've made a hit,' she said, neutrally. She was enormously pleased with Kitty. 'And now, like Prospero, I will give you your freedom. Take that bloody dog and walk. It's a nice afternoon. Tea will be at four-thirty.'

'Can't I help, or something?' asked Kitty.

'You already have,' said Pauline. 'Are you sure those shoes are comfortable? You look terribly smart. We don't dress up much here, you see. Don't get much chance.'

Kitty noticed the small stone sink, the wooden draining board, the dim glass jar containing wild flowers in dirty water on the windowsill. There was no refrigerator, only a larder.

'Pauline,' said Kitty on impulse. 'Let me take you both out to dinner. Your mother would be all right with the two of us. And you ought to get out a bit. I don't like to think of you waiting on me.'

Pauline, who would not normally have contemplated such a thing, thought of the mince she had bought that morning and made a sudden decision to feed it to the dog.

'Well, there is The Manor,' she said slowly. 'That's the local hotel. It's rather smart. I don't think ... '

'Where is it?' asked Kitty. 'Can I walk there and book a table?' And she said it in such an eager tone that Pauline smiled and agreed.

Kitty set off with the dog and the firm intention that they were going to have a really festive evening. It was essential for Pauline to break the pattern, and the old lady, she knew, would enjoy the change of scene. She deserves it, thought Kitty. They both do. And they won't make a move on their own.

She found The Manor, a largish house set in extensive gardens, booked a table for that evening, and then, since she was thirsty from walking, asked if she might have some tea. She was beginning to get the hang of the country, she thought; even the dog followed her without question. They had nothing to say to each other, for Kitty did not believe in wasting words on animals. Or, indeed, in wasting words at all, when every single one counted. She was again reminded of *Adolphe*. Sitting in the garden and sipping her tea, she contemplated the brilliant and frightening future. If everything worked out she might one day find herself seated in her own garden something like this one. Having tea. Her mind veered shyly away from this possibility, but the unrealized thought brought colour to her cheeks and for a while she looked as happy as she supposed herself to be. She scarcely noticed the journey back to the cottage.

'Now, my dear,' said Mrs Bentley, her slice of bread and butter returned somewhat uncertainly to her plate. 'You must tell me what you are doing. I left the field when Existentialism came in, and on the whole I was glad to.'

'But how could you?' cried Kitty. 'It is such a valid creed. I sometimes think it is the only one I can believe in.'

Mrs Bentley hauled out her tin and manufactured another cigarette. 'Well, I thought it was just a desacralized form of Christianity, you know. And rather a poor-spirited one.'

'But that is the point,' said Kitty. 'Because it is desacralized, everyone can join in. There are no elect. There is no grace. It is a system of pure ethics.'

Mrs Bentley smiled faintly. 'And do you understand the idea of the Absurd?' she asked, using the tolerant tone she had formerly employed with students. 'Without recourse to Camus' text,' she added.

Kitty thought. 'It's very difficult. The proposition is that man's natural condition is inherently absurd because he constantly makes assumptions and these assumptions are usually incorrect. Beginnings do not naturally predispose one to good fortune or its opposite. There is therefore no sound basis for reassurance or optimism. All forces are indifferent. And if you don't like the prospect of unlimited free will – and who does? – you can initiate your own sort of rebellion. You can be a "saint without God", as Camus puts it. Though I don't know. One of my students,' she added, 'thinks that Existentialism is a Romantic phenomenon.'

'Oh, but I never doubted it,' said Mrs Bentley in a rather dry tone. She was exhilarated to find herself still ahead of the game. She had to be forcibly reminded twice by Pauline that they were going out that evening, and when she left the room on her daughter's arm, she still had a small triumphant smile on her lips.

When they reassembled, they were on the whole pleased with each other. Pauline had changed into a light wool dress, obviously her best, and Mrs Bentley, rocking slightly in a pair of antique boat-shaped court shoes, wore a silk dress and jacket, into the pockets of which she had stowed her handkerchief and her tin. Pauline was instructed to take the dog next door to the Singletons and had to wake him up to do so. While they waited, Mrs Bentley felt for Kitty's hand. 'Look after my daughter,' she said abruptly. 'I can't do much for her now. When I die I want her to go round the world. Away from this place. I want her to spend all the money at once. Will you see to that?'

Kitty squeezed the hand. 'I promise you,' she said.

The evening was a great success. The hotel was warm and subdued, the tables not too crowded, the windows open on to the deserted garden. Mrs Bentley was persuaded to drink a glass of wine, and whether because of the wine or because of Kitty's promise, she became very animated.

'Mother,' warned Pauline, 'you won't sleep tonight.'

'Who cares?' cried Mrs Bentley, plunging her fork just beyond her apple charlotte and striking the table. 'And if I'm not going to sleep I might as well have some coffee.'

They had coffee and brandy, for Pauline's sake as much as anything, for Kitty was determined that Pauline should sleep. Pauline looked much younger, she noted approvingly; the candlelight flattered her and gave her

86

more colour. She looked, thought Kitty, very English. Shy but invincible. She will be all right, she decided. She will see the world, that I guarantee. She will marry a retired colonial official and settle down in Hong Kong. I shall hear from her once a year – a letter inside a Christmas card, ending 'George joins me in sending his warmest wishes'. I see it clearly.

'This is really very pleasant,' said Mrs Bentley, igniting one of her cigarettes. 'My husband and I used to come here when it was a private house. We knew a lot of people in those days. The Derings. The Granthams. The Bishops.'

Kitty's heart speeded up. 'Oh, yes,' she said casually. 'Maurice Bishop is in the History Department, of course.'

'Maurice was the only son,' mused Mrs Bentley. 'So sad about that marriage of his. Margaret, his mother, was very cut up about it.'

Kitty said slowly, 'You mean the marriage that didn't come off?'

'That's right. Such a pretty girl, too. They were so devoted. We couldn't understand it.'

'Yes, it must have been sad,' said Kitty, in a carefully uninflected voice. Pauline stole a glance at her. 'I thought it was all hushed up.' She meant, I thought it was a secret. I thought that Maurice told only me.

Mrs Bentley laughed rather coarsely. 'That sort of thing never is. Neither of them was terribly reticent, as I remember. Henry Bishop thought it a lot of unnecessary fuss.'

Kitty, who felt suddenly stifled, summoned a passing waiter for the bill. Mrs Bentley, hauled to her feet by Pauline, now seemed to her more ruthless, less sympathetic. Mrs Bentley's teeth, she noted, were as long and as yellow as those of the dog. She felt better when they were outside in the air, densely black, sweet smelling. During the short drive home, Mrs Bentley was still animated. It was clear even to Kitty that she would not sleep that night. She wondered if she would herself.

Upstairs in her tiny bedroom, she walked to the window and shied away instinctively as she saw the new moon through the glass: bad luck for the month to come. Oh, I am misbegotten, she thought. I am not anywhere at home. I believe in nothing. I am truly in an existentialist world. There are no valid prophecies. But then, she thought, breathing deeply in order to calm herself, if I believe in nothing – not in the Bible nor Providence nor Madame Eva – how can I believe that nonsense about the moon?

Suddenly, and for no reason, the dog woke up, whined, prowled round the kitchen, then came up the stairs. He wandered through Pauline's open bedroom door, wandered out again, and sat, panting heavily, outside Kitty's room. With a sigh, she let him in. Gratefully, he fell asleep at once. After a while she was quite glad to have him there.

E I G H T

After Maurice had left, or rather after Kitty surmised that he had left, for there had been no further communication, she found herself suddenly without anything to do. The term had ended and she prepared to wait out the time that remained before her own departure by putting her flat in order and thinking about what to wear. This took exactly half a morning. Instead of bothering with lunch, she wandered down to the little public garden, sat on a bench, and held her face up to the exceptional sun. She was entirely alone. It seemed as good a place to work as any and after a while she took out a book but the sun dazzled and bemused her; she found herself reading the same page twice and eventually she put the book away. She wondered if the story of Paolo and Francesca could be worked into her theory on the Romantic Tradition, and thought about the beautiful sentence she had read in a translation of Dante's account of their fatal kiss: 'that day they read no more'. She imagined a tiny volume tumbling silently to the ground and a hand in a pointed sleeve outstretched. Dante had placed Paolo and Francesca in the circle of the lustful and it was true that the kiss had been rapidly followed by murder, but the story appealed to Kitty. Reading interrupted by kissing and followed by death seemed to her an entirely natural progression.

Two elderly ladies came into view, arm in arm. Their appearance denoted women of the middle class down on their luck; they wore anoraks and headscarves suitable for walking dogs, but old and broken shoes. They sat down on an adjacent bench and one urged the other in a loud voice to remove her coat. 'I don't know,' said the marginally older of the two, shaking a nervous head and fumbling for her bag. 'Oh, for goodness' sake, Mother,' cried the other (her *daughter*, thought Kitty, horrified), 'do make up your mind. Or do you want to sit in the shade? Yes, perhaps that might be better. Over there.' There was another, murmured, hesitation. 'Oh, come on, Mother, do make an effort. Here, I'll take your bag.' The daughter, Kitty noted, had bare legs and wore ankle socks. With infinite slowness they moved off and resettled themselves a dozen paces away. Their new location seemed to present further problems and five minutes later they were back again. Discussion, now rather loud and one-sided, broke out once again as to whether the mother should remove her coat. When she did, it was clearly to please her daughter whom she could not otherwise please, had not ever pleased. And the daughter herself, with her aged embittered face, could not have given much pleasure either, thought Kitty. And both were aware of this and made occasional and futile gestures of conciliation. Like this outing, which neither of them enjoyed. The daughter's angry restlessness was frightening to Kitty who was glad, and by no means surprised, when they decided that the sun was too hot, the garden too lacking in shelter, for them to sit much longer. The coat was put on again, the stick groped for. Roughly, the daughter retied her mother's headscarf. 'All right?' she shouted. 'Better get on, then. No point in hanging about.' From the back, their linked arms, their slow steps, their bent heads indicated closeness, an area of necessary if fatal collusion. But when they had gone, they left a wake of bitterness, a dark stain on the bright day.

At this distance and in this context Maurice took on a superhuman, almost a metaphysical significance for Kitty. His brilliance and ease, his seeming physical invulnerability, the elevated character of his decisions, the distances he covered, his power of choice and strength of resolve, cast him in the guise of the unfettered man, the mythic hero, the deliverer. For the woman whom Maurice would deliver would be saved for ever from the fate of that grim daughter, whose bare white legs and dull shoes, designed perhaps for some antediluvian hike or ramble, continued to register in Kitty's mind's eye. Maurice's choice would be spared the humiliations that lie in wait for the unclaimed woman. She would have a life of splendour, raising sons. Ah! thought Kitty with anguish, the white wedding, the flowers. How can it be me? How could it be me?

These thoughts came rarely but when they came they terrified her with their force. She saw her life, all physical geography removed, as an inexorable progress towards further loneliness. The relics of her past, of that very modest graft that had produced her, had already died away, leaving little trace. More deaths would follow. The silence in Old Church Street, broken only by the sounds of Caroline's radio – but could she even count on Caroline? – would settle in like a long winter. And the Romantic Tradition, growing ever longer and more elaborate, would have to fill her days. I cannot bear it, she thought. I must make it come right, for I shall love no one else. There must be a place left for me, in the gaps left by the cathedrals of France. It must happen soon. She opened her eyes and looked at the sunny deserted garden, heard the sound of the traffic rumbling along the Embankment. *Je joue le tout pour le tout*, she thought.

Her other self, the wise and shrewd self that had come from her grandmother, argued that she had made a good move in deciding to go to France, where she would appear to her advantage, at ease, almost at home. Propinquity, relaxation, meals and conversation shared, would cement their unaltered, their unalterable friendship. And perhaps more. For she had no idea how Maurice felt, had in fact never known. The lightness with which he treated their intimacy had thrilled her with its strangeness, for it was so unlike the brash and noisy attentions of Louise's great-nephew, Jean-Claude, her only other lover. Jean-Claude the insistent, the athletic, the educational partner of her earlier visits to France, the one selected by Louise as a suitable husband. Jean-Claude the student, in his cheap hotel room with the shirt flung to the end of the bed and the remains of a slice of ham curling up in its greasy paper on the rickety table by the window. In vain she would try to entice him out for an evening walk, for a Sunday excursion, for she was sentimental and delicate like her mother. He would look at her in disbelief, would consent only, with much grumbling, to sit at a café for half an hour and drink coffee while she watched the crowds. He was vain, thin, bad-tempered, inexhaustible, and intrusive. He was going to be a brilliant lawyer. He thought it masculine to make a show of jealousy every time she went out, and on her return (for she could not help returning to that hotel room) he treated her as if she had been unfaithful. For a time she had thought his feral energy the most exciting quality in the world. In retrospect it had become devalued by Maurice's delicate and inaccessible secrecy, his silence, the archaic smile which was her after-image of his every visit.

After her last visit to Paris and to Jean-Claude Louise had assessed the situation and had given up her earlier plans for Kitty. Like mother, like daughter, she thought: it will be an Englishman. And she looked with detachment, with the sadness of remembrance, on Kitty's dreamy nature, her willing hard work, her filial visits, even her uncertain appetite – all indications of the same character that Marie-Thérèse had so perfectly inhabited. It will be an Englishman, she had said to Vadim. 'But not yet!' he replied in alarm. Louise shrugged. 'She is twenty-four. But that is all right, for men mature late in this country.' And she had said as much to Kitty, who had every reason to believe her.

But five years had passed since then, and both Kitty and her grandmother had felt an unstated alarm when nothing happened, when the avatar of John Maule failed to materialize and claim his bride. Louise watched, hiding her disappointment, and even when that disappointment hardened into contempt, she still watched. She designed clothes for Kitty and urged her to eat, to put on weight, for Kitty still looked as slight and as virginal as her mother had done. Kitty felt the burden of her grandmother's supervision and knew that although Vadim was delighted to have her still at home, Louise could not wait for her to be gone, so that she could die in peace. For as long as that relic of a daughter remained, Louise must remain to protect her.

Feeling in sudden need of protection in the small sunny stony garden, Kitty rose and turned her steps towards home. She would take her books back to the flat and then visit her grandparents for a cup of tea. In the flat – suddenly dark after the brightness outside – she found a postcard from Maurice, a view of the Christ in Majesty from the tympanum of the west door of Autun. She turned it over quickly. 'Enchanting so far. Have heard some marvellous singing. A bientôt.' His tiny even handwriting affected her like a powerful shock. How I miss him, she thought, when I know he is physically out of my reach. How dull I am without him. But I shall see him soon. *A bientôt.*

Her usual reaction to Maurice was a tremor compounded of fear and longing followed by a mood of intense exhilaration. Waiting by the window, card in hand, for her heart beats to subside, she saw Caroline, in yellow, making her way in the direction, she supposed, of Harrods. A sudden desire to move in crowds, to disperse her tremendous feelings, to share her golden prospects, impelled her towards the telephone. She dialled her grandparents' number. 'Papa,' she said. 'Get ready. We are going out. I shall collect you in a taxi and we shall make a little tour.' Intense silence followed this pronouncement. 'Papa,' urged Kitty. 'There is no need to dress up. We shall simply take advantage of the fine weather and come back when you are tired. Yes, I know she doesn't go out. But she will not have to walk anywhere. And just think how much good it will do her.' She was resolute and saw no reason why she should not be.

When she got to her grandparents' house she saw them from the window of the taxi, waiting for her on the doorstep, their faces stern with anxiety. Vadim, exceptionally, wore a tie, knotted with force and precision, Louise had stoically splashed some powder over her face and changed into a smart but outmoded black silk coat and painful black shoes. She stood, breathing heavily and with some difficulty, her hand under Vadim's arm. He, his brown eyes darting to either side, was eager, nervous, torn between his fear for Louise and his desire to see the shops, the streets, the people whom he so craved and whom he had abandoned without a murmur. 'Maman Louise,' said Kitty, embracing her, 'don't look like that. It is just a little drive. You must not get bored and sit there smoking all day. We will take care of you.' Louise smiled faintly. Kitty took her other hand, pressed it, kissed it. Louise smiled again. '*Vilaine*,' she murmured. And they got into the taxi.

They drove slowly through the brilliant empty afternoon streets of their suburb. They said nothing. Louise sat upright, between them, very straight, a handkerchief clutched in her hand. Vadim and Kitty, on either side of her, stole glances at her from time to time and after a while exchanged congratulatory looks. Louise's breathing steadied, and gradually she relaxed. She saw the buses, the small patient queues, the children coming out of school. Corner shops, an abandoned playground, and then the river, wide and dirty, the city opening out. 'Where would you like to go?' asked Kitty. 'Would you like to go to Kenwood? Or to St James's Park? We could have tea there.' Louise took a long breath, looked at Vadim, looked at Kitty, patted her mouth with her handkerchief which smelt of the violet scent she had always used, and said with a sigh, 'Grosvenor Street.'

In Park Lane, Louise held their hands tightly against the speed and whine of the traffic, then sat up straighter, and began to look intently out of the window. Vadim, his face creased with smiling, made an elaborate gesture of triumph at Kitty. Finally Louise relaxed, lit a cigarette, and assumed something of her old air of dominance, preparing to pass in review what Grosvenor Street had to offer that spring. The brick façade of the house in which they had had the salon was unchanged, but the street was choked with parked cars, and seemed to be more full of men with briefcases than of elegant women. The success of the visit was assured when they saw a young girl emerging from the house. 'Blue jeans!' expostulated Louise. '*Tu vois*, Vadim? Never in my day. And the pullover tied round the waist! Like an artisan!' 'All my students dress like that,' said Kitty. '*Mais c'était une demoiselle*,' protested Louise. '*Mais c'est la dégringolade, quoi?*' She sat up again, superb, her indignation giving her new life. Vadim patted her swollen hand. '*Ma* Louisette, our time was different. Of quality. You were the last. And the best.'

They refused tea, seemed wedded to the hot taxi, in which all the windows had to be kept closed. 'And the foreigners!' said Louise with indignation. Kitty smiled. 'They are tourists,' she assured her. 'And where would you like to go now? It's getting late. We don't want to be caught in the traffic.' Vadim and Louise exchanged a look, and turned to Kitty with supplication in their eyes. 'Percy Street,' they said in unison.

They marvelled at the hot dog and ice cream stands in Park Lane, they shuddered at the thought of the underground car park, they winced at the confusion of cars and buses, they shrank back appalled at the somnambulistic shoppers in Oxford Street. They could not understand how different types of rock music could be blaring from all the doorways at once. '*La dégringolade*,' repeated Louise. In Soho, Vadim screwed up his eyes in ecstasy, imagining the smells, imagining his younger self springing along the pavements. The house in Percy Street was just the same and Kitty ordered the taxi to stop. Suddenly everything seemed quiet, the sunlight fading into a serene and melancholy grey. 'Would you like to walk a bit?' she asked. They did not answer. Their hands were tightly entwined. '*Tu te souviens, ma Louise*?' murmured Vadim. 'Everything,' said Louise, in a voice that Kitty had never heard before. 'I remember everything.'

Kitty left them sitting in the taxi and came back five minutes later with a cake in a cardboard box, a half pound of mushrooms, and some yellow tulips. She had never felt so close to them, to their strange beginnings, their even stranger exile. A red sun was already low on the horizon, signalling the end of the day she had thought would be busy with her own life. Maurice's card was in her bag but she did not think of it. It was impossible to correlate the culture that had produced Giselbertus of Autun, the sculptor of the tympanum on the west door, with the culture that had produced her grandmother – yet they were the same. Kitty felt dizzy with the need to reconcile all these elements: Maurice's France, her grandmother's France, the France of the Romantic Tradition, the France of the greatly desired next two weeks, in which her own fate would be decided. She was tired, she thought; she longed to get home, to sit in her own silent street, and think of herself. For she felt peripheral, felt her personality dissolving in the strong solution of the past, felt her needs to be irrelevant.

Back in the taxi, their hands still clasped, her grandparents seemed at peace. They had little to say on the return journey, and were clearly exhausted by the emotion that had come to them that afternoon. But it had been a necessary exercise, thought Kitty. Here was something to pit against the television serials, the fashion magazines, the concierge's shawl. Here was proof that they had been young, that they had been vigorous and confident; that without them, decline had set in. Thank you, my dear heart, said her grandfather, for a beautiful afternoon. Beautiful, beautiful, said her grandmother.

But on the pavement they seemed very old, stood swaying a little, glad to be home. The quietness of their street, previously despised, was now welcome, and the ghost of Marie-Thérèse required their presence. Kitty helped their slow steps into the house, took Louise's coat, and sat them down. For a while they sat in the darkening room without speaking, too full of remembrance to bother with the present. 'Do you want the television on?' asked Kitty. She looked with love and pity at her surroundings, the grey fake Louis XV tables and chairs with which Louise had furnished her salon and which now stood ranged, in the French style, against the walls. She saw the opaque bowl of the low-watted ceiling light, and the dusty tulle at the windows. In the dark bedroom, she knew, there was a grey fur rug on the bed which remained in place winter and summer. 'Vadim,' said her grandmother, 'let us have a glass of your mixture.' For Vadim brewed a strange and extremely potent plum brandy in a glass jar which stood in the corner of the kitchen. From time to time this exploded, filling the flat with a heady smell which never quite dispersed. It was an excellent restorative, said Vadim, but he could rarely persuade them to drink it.

They sat at the oval table, under the dim ceiling light, the cake unpacked from its box and divided into portions which they ate with spoons. They drank the sticky liqueur from small glasses. The faces of the old people looked drawn in the bad light; they were sombre and impassive, for they had much to think about. Kitty knew that they would go to bed as soon as she left. And now she was very tired herself, longing for a bath and her own bed, where she would read Maurice's postcard over and over again. She cleared her throat. 'You know I am going to Paris next week,' she said. 'I don't know when I shall be back. But I'll telephone every day, as usual.' Louise sighed, and said, 'Wear the grey for travelling. Grey is always correct in Paris.' She seemed listless, uninterested. When Kitty rose to go, leaving them at the table, Louise recovered something of her asperity and examined Kitty. The girl seemed no older than she had done five years ago. But Louise knew that there would be no Jean-Claude on the scene now, and she sensed that there might be someone else. Nothing had been said. But Louise knew the signs: the desire to please, the preoccupation at the back of the eyes, the involuntary half-smile. And the watchfulness, the control. The determination to make the most out of what might be very little. And the evenings when she telephoned very early, as if to get the call out of the way. Louise sensed the love in her grand-daughter, although it seemed to her without an object. No name had been mentioned, no confidences exchanged. Louise thought of her own easy courtship, of her daughter's rapid marriage. It would be different this time, she feared. But with a last ounce of energy, even as she felt the fatigue forcing her lower in the uncomfortable chair, she raised her glass. 'A toast, *ma fille*,' she said. 'A toast. *Que tous vos rêves se réalisent.*' Vadim raised his glass, Kitty hers. '*Que tous nos rêves se réalisent*,' they murmured. Then Kitty kissed them, and left.

N I N E

Kitty wore the grey for travelling, more to please her grandmother than for any other reason. She felt that if she obeyed her in this small particular, Louise would somehow be all right. Her life was governed by small irrational superstitions of this kind.

In the event it did not matter what she wore, for she was alone and quite indifferent to her fellow travellers, whom she perceived as toiling and untidy and rather younger than herself. Some major move was obviously afoot; some school or association was being shifted across the Channel for an extensive holiday of an undefined but educational nature. Large girls, larger than Kitty herself, occupied themselves with amorphous bundles of luggage; they wore waterproof jackets and tennis shoes, and showed a tendency to take sporting kicks at any bundles left in their idiosyncratic path. No one seemed to be in charge of them, and indeed they were very assured, shouting to each other as they boarded the train, manoeuvring their possessions in and out of carriages, flinging themselves down in their seats for an instant and then jumping up to look for their friends or to bawl encouragement out of the window to late-comers. They were rather handsome and their hair did not appear to have been brushed for days. Kitty looked up from her book as a roar of laughter signalled the late appearance of one of their number. The windows suddenly darkened as jerseyed and trousered bodies veered to one side of the train to cheer a grinning red-faced girl bent double under the weight of a towering structure strapped to her back. There was a round of applause as she squeezed through the door. Kitty went back to her book. And we shall have this all over again at the other end, she thought.

But she made an effort to relax, remembering the advice offered to her by Caroline before she left. Kitty, dressed and waiting for the taxi a full hour before she was due to leave had been unable to resist the temptation to ring Caroline's bell to ask her if she looked all right.

'Very nice,' said Caroline unenthusiastically. 'Although, I don't know ... you don't think a bit of colour? You want to arrive looking your best. Is your boyfriend meeting you?'

Kitty blushed. 'I don't even know where he is at the moment,' she confessed. 'He's going to ring me when he gets to Paris.'

Caroline had looked wise. 'Well, don't panic if he doesn't,' she had said. 'And try not to look so anxious. Remember, Kitty, man is the hunter.' And she had smoothed her rather vivid green dress over her bosom, and then examined her nails. She managed to imply that she could deal competently, even expertly, with any problems that Kitty might have wished to confide in her, and that she was available for consultation. But Kitty felt that she had taken enough advice to last her for a very long time, and, with a brief kiss on both cheeks for Caroline she had gone back into her own flat to continue her waiting undisturbed.

Nevertheless, she tried very hard to relax and to appear amiable. They will be students in a year or two's time, she reminded herself, as a deafening game of cards got under way. And the Channel will quieten them down. She was a good sailor, herself.

But she disliked travelling, which always seemed to increase her feeling of isolation, her sense of not belonging in any one clearly defined context. She almost envied the shaggy girls, who looked remarkably like one another, and had clearly been turned out according to some original model by an authoritative committee which knew what that model should be. She felt, as she always felt when the speed of the train increased, that she was losing her sense of identity, that she had forgotten what she looked like, or where she was going. But I am happy this time, she reminded herself; I shall not be alone. Or not for long, anyway. She cheered up, briefly. Then she reached into her bag and pulled out the strip of photographs she had had taken at the station, where she had had to wait for a further half hour for the train to come in. A grey, neat, and unnaturally watchful face, reproduced four times, peered back at her. She sighed, folded the strip over, pushed it back into her bag, and looked out of the window.

Her right arm was nudged, none too gently, and when she turned in its direction it was to find a pleasant and rather highly coloured face, which somehow gave the impression of being as tousled as the immense growth of hair that exploded on all sides of it. It was the girl with the back-pack, which now stood blocking the area between the corridor and the window.

'Excuse me,' said the girl, 'are you French?'

Kitty rehearsed the usual explanation, and then jettisoned it.

'No,' she said, 'but I speak it quite well. Are you in any difficulty?'

'Actually, I wondered if you'd like an apple. My mother loaded me up from her store before I left and

I can hardly move with the weight of them.'

Kitty accepted an apple and asked the girl where they were all going.

'We're camping. My name's Angela, by the way. We're making our way down to Naples.'

Kitty regarded her in consternation.

'You can't camp in Italy,' she said. 'And certainly not in Naples. That's asking for trouble.'

'What on earth do you mean?' The others glanced up from their apples and their cards and their maps and looked at her with genuine curiosity.

'I don't think unaccompanied girls of your age ... '

They roared with laughter.

'We're not unaccompanied, as you put it. The boys have already gone. We've got to meet them in Amiens. And anyway, there's Mr Pascoe.'

At the mention of this name, they doubled up. 'Oh, don't,' moaned the rather pretty girl sitting opposite. 'I can't stand it.'

'Who is Mr Pascoe?' asked Kitty.

'He's with the boys,' explained Angela. 'He's a dream. Clare's in love with him. We shall be too busy fighting over Mr Pascoe to worry about the Italians. My dear, we shan't even notice them.' They shrieked again.

Poor fellow, thought Kitty. Although, I don't know. Maybe he's used to this sort of thing. She was eternally uncertain about standards of behaviour and worried in case she formed or indeed gave a false impression.

'Mr Pascoe is meeting us at Dieppe,' announced Clare dreamily. 'Just think, he'll be on the same train.'

'I must look out for him,' said Kitty. 'He sounds interesting.'

'If you see a tall handsome man with Clare grovelling at his feet, that's Mr Pascoe,' said Angela. 'Look, I must get rid of some of these apples before we get on the boat. Apart from the luggage problem, I want to buy some fags and wine and that and I haven't got room for both.'

'You'd better do it now, then,' urged Kitty. 'We are just coming into Newhaven.' She accepted three more apples and inserted them into her carefully packed grip. Then she stood up, anxious to avoid the flurry of reorganization that would ensue as they tried to get themselves off the train and on to the boat.

'We'll probably see you on the French train,' said Angela. 'We shall have to stay with Clare on the boat because she's going to be sick. Aren't you, Clare?'

'I expect so,' said the pretty girl, picking up another apple and biting into it. 'But I usually get over it quickly enough.'

Nevertheless, though Kitty, I shall sit somewhere else.

The crossing was smooth, the sun warm, the breeze pleasant. Kitty sat on the deck, her book in her lap, mildly restored by the empty scene. The girls had disappeared, below deck, Kitty hoped, and the silence was beneficent. She felt the colour coming back into her face, and as snatches of French came to her through the open window of the saloon, her anxiety disappeared. Again she lifted up her face obediently to the blue sky and tried to capture an extra vigour from the clear air. The time, or rather the timeless interval between the two shores, passed easily and quickly; she was unwilling to move from her place, and lunched neatly on two of Angela's apples.

For the last few minutes of the journey she was joined by a large and handsome French woman with glittering eyes, to whom she nodded a greeting, and who said to her, 'Only five hours of travel and already I am less lucid.' Then as the coast of France came into sharper focus, the woman stood up, shook out her coat, breathed deeply as if inhaling health-giving vapours and announced fervently, *'Enfin. Rien ne vaut la France.'*

Kitty, at this moment, agreed with her. The wider

shore, the wider sky, seemed to promise her a renewal of her powers and of that confidence which, she realized, had become steadily eroded over the past few weeks. She felt as if the Marseillaise should be played and wished that someone had organized it. Picking up her bag she strode to the gangplank, where she found that she had been preceded by the girls, now rather redder in the face, more subdued, and looking more like children, despite their size, than they had on their home ground. Their tragic luggage, more disordered than ever, lay in mountains between herself and the quayside.

'Hello,' said Kitty to the girl who had given her the apples. 'Are you all right? Was your friend sick?'

Angela focused on her with some difficulty. She was, Kitty saw, slightly the worse for wear. 'Oh, hello,' she said vaguely. 'Clare? No, she's fine. We met some chaps in the bar and had a really good time.' She had taken off her waterproof and her jersey to reveal a slightly grubby tee shirt with the face and pointing hand of Lord Kitchener nestling between her redoutable breasts. 'You speak French, don't you? Can you help us get a porter? What does one do? Just yell *Garçon*?'

'Never,' said Kitty, shocked. 'You address them as *Monsieur*. And anyway, I doubt if there will be a porter. You will just have to manage as best you can.' The French woman who had lamented her loss of lucidity looked at them with undisguised dismay. 'But they are drunk,' she hissed at Kitty. *'Mais ce n'est pas permis. Elles ne savent pas se comporter dans le monde.'* Kitty stiffened slightly. 'They are very young, Madame,' she replied in English. The woman looked at her suspiciously, then turned away with a ruffled air. *'Tout de même,'* she murmured. 'Silly cow,' remarked Clare, thus revealing herself as the trail blazer of the group. Hoots and shrieks of laughter began to reassert themselves as the girls, and Kitty, manoeuvred their luggage down the gangplank, on to the platform, and into the waiting train. From time to time the cortège broke down, until at one point Clare and Angela collapsed on the platform, clinging to each other, helpless, until urged by Kitty to stagger the rest of the way. To their original bundles were now added carrier bags filled with bottles and cartons of cigarettes. Kitty herself was blamelessly neat.

Inside the train the girls fell instantly and unanimously asleep and thus did not see a tall sardonic looking man in an open-necked shirt peering in from the corridor. Kitty edged the door open and looked at him enquiringly. She felt responsible for the girls. 'Pascoe,' he announced, in a low and bitter voice. 'Are they all here?' She nodded. He nodded too, shut the door, and disappeared. Five minutes later he reappeared, opened the door, and said, 'There is a buffet car at the other end. I think we both need a cup of coffee. They won't wake up until we get to Paris,' he added. 'And then, God help me.'

'Why should God help you?' asked Kitty as they edged their way round a small metal table and sat down. 'They seem rather nice.'

'Because,' he said, even more bitterly, 'we are to spend the night in an hotel near the Gare du Nord. They will be trying to escape all night, to see the sights, as they call it. You can imagine how plentiful those are around the Gare du Nord. They will want night clubs and champagne and they will eat all the wrong things. And to think I might be walking in the Dolomites, as I originally planned.' He sighed theatrically.

He had, Kitty decided, a Byronic head, a fact of which he was well aware, as he kept turning his head aside so as to present himself in three-quarter profile. He was remarkably handsome and she could understand why Clare was in love with him. She did not, however, rate

Clare's chances very highly; Mr Pascoe seemed to have enough to do just to cope with himself.

'You don't look like a schoolmaster,' she ventured to remark.

'I have a bad leg,' was his obscure reply. That is simply not true, thought Kitty. You read that in a novel about the First World War. She blushed slightly at this evidence of bad faith on her part.

'Wouldn't that have held you up in the Dolomites?' she asked.

'Not at all,' he said, sharply. 'If I don't exercise, it gets very stiff. And all the exercise I shall get this holiday is watching tents being put up and dismantled.' He shook his handsome head and looked so genuinely disgusted that Kitty felt a little sorry for him. The girls, after all, had been rather overpowering and she had only known them for the inside of a day. And there were the boys to consider, too.

'Have you done this job for long?' she asked.

'Only for a couple of terms,' he replied. 'I didn't do much of anything before that, apart from a bit of farming for my father. Then I got involved in a car smash and it set me back in all sorts of curious ways and the chap at the hospital was a friend of the head of this school and they wanted a temporary replacement so I let myself be persuaded. It's been hell,' he added simply. 'I shall leave at the end of the year. With relief.'

So he really has got a bad leg, thought Kitty, with a sense of shame. And the chap at the hospital was evidently a doctor. Perhaps something did go rather wrong with Mr Pascoe.

'I'm a teacher too,' she said. 'I quite like it.'

He took no notice of this. 'The kids aren't too bad,' he said. 'In fact I get on better with them than I do with the so-called adults.'

My dear, thought Kitty, you probably always will.

107

You have not looked at me once since we sat down. Which is a pity because you seem nice and interesting and you are extraordinarily good-looking and I think I might begin to enjoy your company very much. If only you weren't so impossibly self-absorbed. A Romantic hero, she decided. And with the limp to go with it.

She said none of this but watched his sulky handsome face and the long fingers wrapping and unwrapping the same piece of sugar. As she was studying him – and he really was rather remarkable – he surprised her by raising his eyes and gazing at her critically. They both felt a slight sense of shock and continued to look at each other, with the blood rising in their cheeks, until, reluctantly, Mr Pascoe turned his eyes away and concentrated on wrapping his lump of sugar again.

After a moment he cleared his throat. 'You would be doing me a service if you would have dinner with me tonight,' he said, carelessly.

Kitty smiled. 'With the girls?' she asked.

'After the girls are in bed,' he replied. 'I really cannot be responsible for them after that. I can't lock them in, after all. And I can't stand outside their rooms waiting to catch them.'

'I wonder why they didn't send a woman teacher,' said Kitty.

'They did, but she was called home suddenly. Her mother fell and broke a hip. Which sounds like a long job.'

'Cheer up,' said Kitty, who did not normally say such things. 'At least the weather is good. You won't have too bad a time. And I don't mind helping you with the girls this evening, if it will make any difference. We could both take them out.' She felt that this was an acceptable suggestion, but he did not seem noticeably pleased with it. 'What they would probably like,' she went on, 'is that self-service place in the rue de Rivoli.

They can have chicken and chips. I dare say they will be very tired when they have eaten. We can take them back on the Metro, and you can relax after that. With your bad leg,' she added.

He brooded. He was, Kitty saw, too proud to try to persuade her. And too used to getting his own way with women to acknowledge that she had deflected him from his original purpose. Which is a pity, she thought again. I might have enjoyed having dinner with him. It would have filled in this evening. But supposing Maurice is already there? Supposing there is a telephone message waiting for me at the hotel? I shall have to go there straight away, as soon as we get to Paris. And then, if there is no message, I can arrange to meet them all in the rue de Rivoli. But I must go straight back to the hotel afterwards, in case Maurice telephones.

She raised her eyes from this calculation to find him staring at her again, and again she blushed slightly.

'Are you meeting someone in Paris?' he asked.

'In a way,' she said. She did not want to offend his pride any further. 'It's a colleague, really,' she went on, rather hesitantly, as his face darkened. 'We are going to look at some cathedrals together.'

'A male colleague?' he asked.

Kitty thought of Maurice, driving through France, alone, without her, and felt a touch of sadness. I could have been with him all the time, she thought.

'Yes, oh yes,' she said hurriedly, for she felt the onset of one of her bleak moods.

'You're very pretty,' he said, and looked annoyed with himself for having conceded so much. He had obviously been handsome from infancy and had long been used to the idea of the superiority of his own looks and appearance.

Kitty smiled. 'Thank you,' she murmured, then, turning to look out of the window, exclaimed, in genuine surprise, 'But we are nearly there! I have never known a journey to go so quickly!'

He sighed, with genuine heaviness. It can't be much fun for him, she thought. 'Mr Pascoe,' she said, 'would you like me to help you with the girls this evening? I could meet you at the self-service place. I just want to see if my friend has left a message for me at the hotel first.'

He turned his face to the window, and stayed in that position for a moment, exhibiting his profile.

'Sweet of you,' he said finally. 'Would seven-thirty be too early? I expect they will need a wash, or something. And I had better get the rooms sorted out.'

She smiled again. 'Seven-thirty in the rue de Rivoli, then. We had better get back to them, I suppose.'

They lurched through the train with difficulty, for the corridor was already jammed with people and luggage. In the carriage the girls were awakening from their sleep, yawning and dishevelled. They looked younger and dirtier than ever, but, Kitty noted, they recovered all the more quickly because of their youth.

'We're all having dinner together,' Kitty informed them. At that moment Mr Pascoe loomed behind her, and Clare's face registered astonishment. 'I will see you all at the barrier,' said Mr Pascoe. 'Wait until everybody has got off before you attempt to move that luggage. And be as quick as you can.'

'I'll say goodbye now,' Kitty told them, picking up her grip. 'But I shall see you all later. I just want to see if there is a message for me at my hotel. Are you all right? You don't feel sick, do you, Clare?'

'I am perfectly all right, thank you,' Clare replied in a repressive tone of voice. She will be a formidable woman in a couple of years' time, thought Kitty, and she turned her attention to finding a taxi, for now her mind was on what awaited her at the hotel, and she had

110

almost forgotten that the girls existed.

As the taxi jerked through the early evening traffic she fell into a dream. Supposing that Maurice had in fact already arrived? She somehow was sure that he was there, that she would see him very soon, that they would spend the whole of the next two weeks together, and that life would be irremediably changed by this fact. She did not notice the beautiful evening, for her gaze was turned inwards, and she held her head still, using the tall slices of building sliding by on either side of her as blinkers, shutting out that part of the world that was irrelevant to her preoccupations. She gave herself over to the business of anticipation, for she suspected that she might need to become rather good at doing so. Paris seethed past her unnoticed as she tried to remember whether or not she had given Maurice her telephone number. She had told him the name of the hotel and where it was. Oh, this is ridiculous, she said to herself. He probably called in and left a note, telling me where to find him.

But there was no message waiting for her. Rather slowly she went up the stairs and unlocked the door of her room. She walked to the window as if she might see him coming. Then she sat on the bed for a few minutes. Eventually she sighed and stood up and started to unpack; she washed her face and brushed her hair, and then, when she could put it off no longer, she went down the stairs again and out into the cooling evening, and made her way to the rue de Rivoli, for chicken and chips, with Mr Pascoe, and the girls.

T E N

The sort of hotel which Kitty thought it appropriate to afford on this occasion had rooms which were neither warm enough nor light enough. In the daytime she managed to forget these very slight irritations, for there was plenty to see and to do, and she had had many useful ideas for her work. But she hated going back in the evenings, had developed a dread, more acute than the ennui of Old Church Street, of sitting alone, with her books, when she had so much to say, so many ideas to offer. She was full of words and she had to keep them all to herself. After dinner, eaten at a bistro on the corner of the street, a sadness which she did not fully comprehend, set in, and the thought of sitting at a small table under a weak light in a bedroom furnished in shades of tired crimson, while she grappled with the task of writing her lecture, an exercise which she found easy in the daytime and impossible in the evenings, came to be associated in her mind with the thought of solitude, of exile. Exile, she thought. I have felt this before. But she could not remember in what context.

She was usually in bed by nine. Trying to read, under an even weaker light, she forced herself to ignore the fact that Maurice had not telephoned and that there had been no message waiting for her. She had been installed for a week. Every morning she took great pains with her appearance, in case he should have arrived without telling her. Every morning she informed the woman at the desk of the hotel when she would be back, after her day's reading and walking. 'I am expecting a message,' she said. By now they all knew this, and shook their heads sympathetically in the evenings when she returned. She knew that such humiliation was not the normal lot of women who were loved, and although she schooled herself to remember that Maurice never made plans very far ahead, that he frequently got dates wrong, and that in any case he did not know – must not know – that she waited with such intensity for a sign from him, a disappointment had insinuated itself into her and she knew that it would not easily be dislodged.

So that when he finally telephoned, she was almost dull with anticlimax and answered him slowly. 'Did I wake you up?' he said. 'I'm exhausted myself.' 'Where are you?' was all she wanted to know. 'In an enchanting little hotel just outside Chartres,' he said. He sounded not at all tired. 'I've just had the best meal of my life. And the cathedral's floodlit, it's quite perfect. Listen, Kitty. I could be with you tomorrow for lunch. I want one last look in the morning. I could pick you up at your hotel around one. You'll have time to have your hair done, my love.'

She shrank back against the headboard of the old-fashioned bed and tried to assess the situation. Where was he going to stay in Paris? He had said nothing about that. He had sounded airy, almost euphoric. And he had called her 'my love'. Surely that meant something? Her endearments to him, which she had had to curtail because she knew that he would not welcome any show of fervour on her part, were always irrepressible and sincere. She thought that this was how the matter should be. Words meant such a very great deal to her – and more than that, information conveyed by means of

113

words – that she wanted them to mean a great deal to everyone else. For some reason she thought of her student Mr Mills and his clumsy translations. You are accurate, she had told him, and yet you are not very near the meaning. Aim at both. This way you are losing a great deal of the available information. You are eliding it. He had looked at her uncomprehendingly: he had always been perfectly satisfied with his own translations.

Enough of this, she thought. It is important that I sleep well tonight, that I look well tomorrow. I will have my hair done, although it was done only two days ago. The lecture can wait. I am on holiday, she reminded herself. And Maurice will be here tomorrow. I shall see him at last and we shall be together. We shall get in the car and go to Saint-Denis. Nevertheless she did not sleep well.

She was ready and waiting by ten o'clock the next morning, and only the repeated knocks of the chambermaid got her out of her room, for she would have been content just to sit there until he arrived. She wandered haphazardly through the uninteresting streets of her immediate district, unwilling to venture far, her own plans and wishes suspended. The sunshine of the previous weeks had given way to a grey humidity which was not unpleasant but which imparted a slight feeling of unreality. She was now in a world of low definition. The previously acute angles made by the streets were softened, blurred; even sounds were more remote. And although it was morning it felt like afternoon, as if the weather had brought with it a prolonged siesta. Kitty Maule sat drinking a cup of coffee with precise and deliberate gestures. Nothing in her appearance indicated strain. She wanted, quite perversely, given the boredom of the preceding week, to get on with her work. This was, in fact, she had to admit, something of an error of timing. And she did not know how long she would be staying or how much time she had left.

She went back to the hotel to change her shoes and repair her appearance, and when she had done these things she simply sat at the window and waited. She heard twelve o'clock strike, and then, much earlier than she had expected, she saw Maurice. He was wearing a blue checked shirt and his scarlet pullover and he was carrying an armful of books. He looked as if he had just emerged from the library after a peaceful morning's work, but he was in fact coming towards her hotel. He could not see her, and because he could not see her she rushed down the stairs and out into the street so that they could meet face to face.

He kissed her lightly on both cheeks. He looked very well, even tanned. 'Oh, come in quickly and tell me all about it,' she said. 'Let me leave these books at the desk,' he said, 'and let's get something to eat. I'm absolutely starving.' Oh, but I am a fool, thought Kitty, looking at his long brown hands. I should have booked him a room here. Where are my wits? But maybe he did that on the telephone, last night. In which case, why does he not bring his books upstairs? 'Maurice,' she urged, 'won't you stay here?' and she put her hand lovingly on his.

'But I'm just round the corner, my love. At the Franklin Roosevelt, no less. But I couldn't get a room with a bath. Have you got a bath, Kitty? Darling, can I have a bath later?' So it will have to be love in the afternoon, thought Kitty. *Merde, alors.*

My love. Darling. Kitty took more nourishment from these words, and from the sight of Maurice's teeth biting into a plateful of radishes, than she did from her own tomato salad, to which she referred abstractedly from time to time. She took an inventory of his lowered eyelashes, his pale brown skin, his careful hands. Then she switched their plates so that he could finish her tomato salad, as she knew he wanted to do, and took more bread and gave it to him. Her earlier disappointments had faded from her mind and she could only concentrate on what she had in front of her: Maurice, captive, his mouth limpid with oil.

A little while later, she said, 'Where did you leave the car?' By this time he was carefully stripping the meat from a chop. 'Gone on ahead,' he answered. 'I found someone to drive it back for me. Are you going to eat your potatoes, Kitty?' She handed over her plate. His physical presence so bemused her that her own awakened appetite seemed subsumed into his. He was eating for them both, and that was how she would have it. To feed him, at that moment, was all she wanted to do; the food was enhanced by his enjoyment of it and she speared a potato from his plate because it looked so much more appetizing than when it had previously featured on her own. A man at the next table, eating alone, smiled faintly at her absorption; she caught his eye, and smiled back. Across Maurice's bent head they looked at each other gravely and with complete understanding. I love him, you see, she said, without uttering a word. The man sighed, called for his bill, and raised his coffee cup to her. Yes, she thought, luck. I have it at last. When she turned her head to Maurice, she found him smiling at her. 'Why, Kitty,' he said, 'I believe you are misbehaving.'

'Right,' he continued, looking at his watch. 'Now how do we get to Saint-Denis? In a train, I suppose. A dreary little train from the Gare du Nord.'

'Oh, but Maurice,' she protested. 'We don't have to go today, do we? I thought you wanted a bath.'

'I can have one when we come back. And yes, we do have to go today, my love, because I have to fly home in the morning.'

116

'But Maurice ... '

'I know, I know. It's a bore, but my godmother's coming to stay, and I promised my parents. So you see, Kitty, there is not a moment to lose.'

In the train he dropped lightly off to sleep, his head cradled in his hand. When she turned her head away from watching him she looked out of the window, a smeared hopeless window, on to a landscape of high-rise flats, small factories, complicated overhead electrical connections. The rumbling suburban train was filled with slight dark-skinned men in eccentric hats, looking furtive yet business-like, their belongings, in cardboard suitcases, kept firmly between their knees. Kitty felt nervous and woke Maurice up. 'Please don't relax too much,' she pleaded. 'I shall never know when we ought to get off. It all looks the same. It is probably the same as this all the way to the coast. It always is when you go north.' He looked at her mildly. His brief sleep seemed to have subdued him, made him into the controlled and inaccessible creature she had always known, without that effervescent lightness, that ... that *jauntiness*, yes, that was what it was, that he had shown ever since he had arrived. Only three hours ago, she marvelled. And he must have been as excited as I was. Then why can't he stay? Why won't he stay?

Her very slight melancholy increased during the walk to the basilica, which she perceived as a dungeon surrounded by abattoirs. The grey afternoon cast a bad light on what was already unprepossessing: a street filled with inexpensive shops, horse-meat butchers, launderettes. Several stuporose figures sat slumped in the Bar des Sports. Outside a café a waiter in shirtsleeves and a long black apron stood yawning. The day had darkened and a light rain was falling. He will get his lovely pullover wet, she thought, as they stumbled over the greasy cobbles to the façade of the west front.

117

She was very disappointed with what she saw. The rose window was mean, the stone neither properly weathered nor entirely clean, the single tower heavy and graceless. The carving of the central portal was in such low relief that she felt as if she were looking at something executed in metalwork. Above the main door, which was firmly and inexorably closed, sat a sculpted Christ in Majesty, of indeterminate age, His arms prolonged by scrolls proclaiming His glory. Above Him, tiny figures of saints, angels, and doctors of the church wheeled round the semi-circular archivault, meeting in head-on collision above His head. 'Maurice,' said Kitty longingly, 'there seems to be a fine eighteenth-century building to our right. Couldn't we look at that?' She craved something elegant and rational, something that would allow her to keep her balance, for Saint-Denis, she felt, contained the unreason of God, and the Christ figure seemed to bar the door to her unworthiness. Maurice, his eyes uplifted to the Christ, ignored her question; he stood transfixed, in the rain, his hair darkened by the damp drizzle, while she darted in the side door for shelter.

Inside, for a while, she could see nothing, could only hear footsteps, did not know if Maurice had followed her. She was in a vast necropolis, an indoor cemetery reserved for the rich, the famous, and the very dead. She could hear the voice of a guide, somewhere ahead of her, although she could not make out anyone else in the building. She supposed that the voice was a recording. An inexplicable feeling of dread made her linger near the door. Maurice, distinguishable by his red pullover, seemed somehow to have got in front of her. He was quite oblivious to her presence, or had forgotten it, and she was too uncertain of herself to inflict it on him.

After a while she began to wander fearfully among the tombs. She was momentarily diverted by the beauty of

118

the names: Dagobert, Childebert, Carloman, Frédé-
gonde, Ermentrude, Blanche of Castille, Isabelle of
Aragon. Little by little, her acute unease left her and she
dared to look at the sculpture, referring to her
guidebook to see if she were going the right way about
it. The tomb of Dagobert I was like a well-ordered linen
cupboard, with rows of figures placed on shelves and
Dagobert stowed away neatly underneath them. Around
the tomb of Louis de Valois marched tiny figures in
hooded cloaks, doing their work of mourning for the
dead. That same prince, lying flat but not quite dead, his
eyes open, his hands raised in prayer, gave her pause;
she saw on his Gothic face something of the intransi-
gence and the integrity of the faith that she had glimpsed
in Maurice. But Blanche of Castille was very definitely
dead, so flat that she did not even inhabit her fine dress
with the goffered edging, her empty head now at one
with her metal crown in mineral consistency.

Kitty was oddly disquieted by the coupled kings and
queens, not necessarily man and wife, who lay together
as on a bed, an eternal marriage bed. Discreetly clothed,
Carloman (died 771, said her guidebook) lay next to
Ermentrude, and Philippe (died 1131) next to Con-
stance of Castille. There was a look of intimacy, of
informality, for all their robes, crowns and sceptres.
Kitty, in the darkening church, walked back, turned a
corner, walked on, and caught her breath. In front of
her she saw the soles of four bare feet and the fore-
shortened nude bodies of two very recognizable human
beings. Under a marble catafalque lay two marble
figures, caught, apparently, at the moment of their
dying, the man's chest arched, his toes separated with
anguish, his hand protecting his genitals; the woman
limper, but with braced knees and curling toes. Kitty
looked at her guidebook: Henry II and Catherine de
Medici, by Germain Pilon. On top of the catafalque, in

119

bronze, were kneeling statues of the King and Queen as they had been in life: the woman graceful, accomplished, with pearls in her hair, the man heavy, eloquent, clever, a long political hand outstretched. Kitty returned to the *gisants*, the dead figures. This was the reality, then. Death. And yet a death that seemed almost acceptable if one had a companion. Henry and Catherine, their agony shared, were familiar with the disgraces of each other's bodies. They had not been idealized: the woman's breast was flat and her legs plump. Apart from their curling toes, they might have been asleep on any night of their lives.

Now Kitty could see Maurice, his red pullover the only colour in the gloom. There was no one but themselves in the huge building. She listened, as if taken back in time, for the confident footsteps of the faithful. There were none. She searched for a candle to light to Marie-Thérèse and could not find one: this was a church for members only. Then she saw Maurice sink to his knees in front of the statue of the Virgin by Dagobert's tomb and watched his bent head as he prayed. He has left me, she thought; I am alone, and she leaned against a pillar, her throat aching. She tried to pray and failed. Then she said, silently, Marie-Thérèse, dearest little mother, are you there? Is this what you wanted for me, your heart's darling, on those evenings calm enough to quiet even your fears, when we walked together arm in arm in the tiny garden? Do you see him, my pious lover, for whom I wait in hotel rooms, whose notes I type, whose dinners I cook, and who will never marry me? He prays to the Madonna, a stone lady with a chipped face. Do you watch me, the daughter who amazed and alarmed you sometimes with her strange ambitions? Did you wish for something simpler, more docile, more predictable? You did not hand me on, as a parent should, but you were so scarcely a parent. You were a child, and perhaps all the children I shall ever have. Have you found him again, your husband, the father I never knew? Will you tell him who I am? You, so happy to be looked after by others, will you try to look after me?

After a while she blotted her eyes carefully, and repaired her appearance as best she could. Maurice now came towards her, his mild smile restored. He seemed untouched by fatigue or doubt. The business of living is so simple for him, she thought, and she watched him as, hands on hips, he surveyed the capitals of the columns. She peered at her watch in almost total darkness. 'Maurice,' she said urgently, 'it's very late. Let's go home now. I hate this place.' He frowned slightly. 'How can you?' he said. 'I could stay here for hours.' 'But you are going back tomorrow,' she pleaded. 'We have so little time together.' With a sigh he reached out a long arm and rested it on her shoulder and looked searchingly into her face. 'All right, Kitty,' he said. 'We'll go home now.'

On the way back he was silent. From time to time he pulled out a small notebook and wrote something down. She felt as if she had been importunate, was left with a small area of discomfort in her mind. But I am mad, she thought. It is simply that our earlier unity was broken. This is quite natural. People take some time to come together again. And Saint-Denis was not perhaps the best place for us. I hope I haven't ruined his lecture.

Back in her room she recovered her earlier good spirits. She had had some tea sent up, and she watched him striding about, with his cup in his hand, his ring just glinting beneath the saucer. He had taken off his wet pullover and shoes, and stood still, from time to time, abstracted, half-dressed, until she urged him to drink. She had slipped next door to the cake-shop and bought two apple chaussons and two croissants filled with

121

almond paste. They ate ravenously, their mouths perfumed with the sweet mixtures. When they kissed, they exchanged identical breaths, and she made a vow that she would never forget that particular taste as long as she lived.

While he lay in the bath, she sat at the window and looked into the wet street. It was raining hard now and she could see the lights reflected in deep puddles. She lit a cigarette – the first of the day, she noticed with surprise – and sat there becalmed. She felt herself assuming a more noble shape in the chair, envisaged her head as smaller, neater, her feet more graceful than usual. She looked round the small crimson room, its ugliness now masked by the dim lamps and the sight of Maurice's clothes on the bed. 'Where shall we eat?' she called out to him. She heard him step out of the bath and pad towards her. 'Kitty,' he protested. 'What is the matter with you suddenly? You want to do everything at once.'

They ate at a small obscure restaurant near the hotel, for the rain had now settled in for the night. This time it was she who was hungry and he who watched her. She was flushed and animated; she took small pieces of meat on her fork and put them on his plate. He was rather silent, had completely lost his earlier ebullience. She supposed that the afternoon in the basilica had reawakened in him thoughts of God and death and memories of his tragic time and hopes for ... For what, exactly? Did Maurice have any hopes? If he did, she did not know what they could be. With confidence and the right assumptions, thought Kitty Maule, I dare say you don't need to live on faith at all. As, oddly enough, I do.

They parted early, earlier than she had expected. In the vestibule of her hotel he rested his arms on her shoulders and looked at her again, his face stripped of its habitual masking smile. It was a time of extreme

122

gravity for both of them. Neither of them spoke, and the moment, prolonged, silent, seemed endless, irreversible, of momentous significance. Finally she said, in a voice that she tried to make as light as possible, 'You are tired, my darling. Go and get some sleep.' He leaned his forehead against hers, seemed about to say something, then stood up with a sigh. 'Goodnight, Kitty,' he said, and went out into the rain.

E L E V E N

'Did you enjoy France, Miss Maule?' asked Mills politely.

'Very much, thank you,' Kitty replied. 'By the way, I hope you managed to go yourselves?'

'I didn't,' said Larter. 'I got a job on a building site. Made a bomb.' The others smiled. Miss Fairchild had replaced her pullover with a crumpled cotton blouse. Otherwise nothing had changed.

They were all the better for a break, Kitty decided. They looked fitter, had lost their winter pallor, had even become quite tanned in the sun that now broke into their little room and swirled motes of dust in a shaft that plunged from the window in front of her to the bookshelves behind her, glancing off the heads of Larter and Mills and irradiating Miss Fairchild's long crepey hair. It was their last meeting and it was unlikely that they would ever come together again.

Kitty cleared her throat. 'This is our last meeting, as you know,' she said, 'and I thought we might do two things today. We'll take a final look at *Adolphe* and see if the end of the novel is consonant with the beginning. And then we might ask ourselves what it tells us about the Romantic hero as an entity, a phenomenon. Or indeed if there is such a thing as the Romantic hero, or whether it is an archetype set up by the Romantics

124

themselves. Who would like to start?'

'The thing that struck me,' said Larter, 'was that when I read the novel again I could visualize the end far more easily than I could the beginning.'

Kitty smiled. 'Would you explain?' she asked.

He reflected briefly. 'It all goes on in this rather mournful manner and you can't see why it should ever end. The descriptions ... ' He nodded his head to Kitty. 'You were right. The *words* give this very impression. They are absolutely colourless. They describe very violent emotions but they are absolutely colourless. Abstract.'

'Do you find that this works for or against the tenor of the story?' asked Kitty.

'Against,' said Mills.

'For,' said Larter.

'You disagree with the effect as it stands, Philip?' asked Kitty. 'Jane?'

'I don't like the book,' said Miss Fairchild.

'That is your prerogative,' allowed Kitty, 'but you will have to tell us why you feel this way. Can you do that?' There was a pause, while they waited for a pronouncement. Then Larter could be restrained no longer.

'To go back to what I was saying. I *visualize* the end, which I would not be able to do if the beginning were not kept absolutely, rigorously neutral.'

'Examples, please,' said Kitty.

'Well, after Adolphe has decided to leave Ellénore and writes to his horrible friend, telling him of his resolve, and after the letter has fallen into Ellénore's hands, she becomes ill.'

'It is a very imprecise illness,' murmured Kitty.

'Yes, it's clearly a fictional device and not very well handled. But after *that*, they go for a walk. A last walk, because she's obviously dying. And the author actually and for the first time refers to the scenery.'

125

Mills searched his text. 'He simply says it was one of those winter days with pale sunshine ... no leaves on the trees ... no birds. I don't call that much of a description.'

Kitty smiled. 'You obviously want the author to write it differently. You want another book altogether. So does Jane.' Miss Fairchild nodded and started to wind a long strand of hair around her finger.

'The point is,' Larter almost shouted, 'that in the course of this walk that you find so uninteresting, there is a sound, and that is the dimension that has been missing from the words so far.'

'Good,' said Kitty. 'Go on.'

'Well, Adolphe, in the course of this walk, which lasts a mere paragraph, no doubt to your disappointment' – he addressed these words to Mills – 'hears nothing but icy grass *creaking* under their feet.' He stopped dramatically.

Mills removed his glasses. 'I don't see anything remarkable in that,' he said.

'Oh, I think it is significant rather than remarkable,' said Kitty. 'For the first time we are aware of the author's consciousness rather than his recital. The gap between the writer and the reader is closing. And in the end it breaks down altogether.'

'I find the ending quite unsatisfactory,' said Mills. 'If only he had just let her die. But he can't leave it alone. He has to find a posthumous letter. And then he has to pretend to be somebody else, writing to an editor and saying he has found the manuscript and would it be worth publishing. And then the editor has to write back saying yes, but he doesn't think it will do any good.' Mills shook his head. 'Surely this is very clumsy?'

'It is clumsy as fiction, but by this time the author is no longer writing a novel. He is trying to distance something that happened and from which he cannot recover. Can you tell me the point at which this becomes apparent?'

Larter expelled a jet of smoke, removed his long stained finger from between the pages of his book, and imposing silence with his hand, intoned, '"It was no longer the regret for love, it was a feeling both sadder and more sombre: love so identifies itself with the loved object that there is a sort of charm even in despair."' He broke off. 'Is that it?' he asked Kitty.

'Almost,' she replied. 'But you started too early. Go on.'

' " . . . I did not wish to die with Ellénore; I was going to live without her in this desert of a world that I had so often longed to inhabit independently. I had broken with the one who loved me; I had broken that heart, companion of my own, which persisted in its devotion to me, in its untiring tenderness; already isolation engulfed me." That's it,' he nodded, almost to himself.

'Go on,' said Kitty.

' "Ellénore was still alive, but I could no longer confide my thoughts to her; I was already alone in the world; I no longer lived in that atmosphere of love that she diffused around me; the air that I breathed seemed harsher to me, the faces of the people that I met more indifferent; the whole of nature seemed to tell me that I should never again be loved." '

'Psychiatrists call this phenomenon "separation anxiety",' said Kitty. 'It is more widespread than you suppose. Sociologists blame the alienating effects of modern urban life. But Adolphe is on an estate in the middle of Poland: he suffers the disorder in its pure state. Alienation is a Romantic phenomenon. Do you see what Adolphe says towards the very end of the book? Philip?'

' "How it weighed on me, that liberty I had longed for! How my heart missed that dependence which had

127

so frequently repelled me! Formerly all my actions had an aim; with each of them I was sure either to avert pain or to give pleasure. I complained of this; I was impatient that a loving eye should watch my every move, and that the happiness of another should be of so much consequence. Now nobody watched me; I was of interest to nobody; nobody claimed my time or my attention; no voice called me back when I went out. I was free indeed, I was no longer loved; I was a stranger to the rest of the world."'

'"To everyone,"' corrected Kitty. 'He means that he has lost that intimacy with one person that he had so resented. But it also means that he has entered into a state of alienation.'

'Then I was right,' said Larter, 'when I talked about Existentialism.'

'You were right in a certain sense,' said Kitty. 'But you must not project forwards. Constant is not an existentialist. The only way he can get out of his dilemma is to deliver a blanket moral condemnation of Adolphe's conduct through the person of "the editor".' In her clear voice she read, '"*La grande question dans la vie c'est la douleur que l'on cause, et la métaphysique la plus ingénieuse ne justifie pas l'homme qui déchire le cœur qu'il aimait. Je hais, d'ailleurs, cette fatuité d'un esprit qui croit excuser ce qu'il explique; je hais cette vanité qui s'occupe d'elle-même en racontant le mal qu'elle a fait, qui a la prétention de se faire plaindre en se décrivant, et qui, planant indestructible au milieu des ruines, s'analyse au lieu de se repentir.*" He is very scrupulous, you see,' she added. 'He allows himself no extentuating circumstances.'

'Neither do the existentialists,' said Larter.

They paused, exhausted, even faintly disgusted, by the book. Outside in the corridor came the sound of footsteps, a cough, a burst of laughter, the footsteps dying

128

away. It was very warm. The afternoon, Kitty realized, was not going well.

'What about sex?' demanded Larter, splitting a match with his thumbnail. 'Are these two lovers, or what? Or is it all over between them?'

'We are not meant to know that,' said Kitty. 'They are certainly in thrall to each other. But sometimes, you see,' she said with an intimation of distress, 'romantic love can lead to disastrous fidelities. Or indeed ultimately to chastity,' she added.

Miss Fairchild's large and slanted eyes slid towards Kitty as if expecting her to expand on this point. Then her eyes slid round to Mills and dropped to look at his watch. She never wore one herself. Then, sweeping her hair briskly behind her neck, she pronounced that she thought Adolphe was mad.

'That is very interesting,' said Kitty, rallying. 'In the eighteenth century his symptoms would certainly have been diagnosed as a form of madness. They knew all about morbid sensitivity then. It was an entirely negative characteristic, regarded as bad luck, the result of being unfortunately born, as Diderot put it. Why, then, does it assume such immense importance in the first third of the nineteenth century? Jane?'

'Something to do with the loss of faith?'

Suddenly, into Kitty's mind, came an image of the interior of a Gothic church. She saw herself sitting alone in a pew, with candles burning somewhere to her right, and she heard footsteps in the background. She remembered feeling intolerable loneliness in such a situation. And yet, she thought, I should be intellectually dishonest if I represented this feeling as the one that crippled Adolphe.

'I do not think that Adolphe ever lost his faith,' she replied to Miss Fairchild. 'Because I do not think he ever found it in the first place. I think he supposed that

129

reason would carry him through. Although he behaves in an unreasonable manner, his actual reasoning processes work overtime.'

'That is probably what is wrong with him,' said Larter.

'Yes, but it is characteristic of the Romantic to reason endlessly in unbearable situations, and yet to remain bound by such situations. Take any example you care to mention, fact or fiction. And it still obtains today. For the Romantic, the power of reason no longer operates. Or rather, it operates, but it cannot bring about change.'

'That makes sense,' conceded Mills. 'In the eighteenth century they thought that change could only come about by the operation of reason.'

'And then this awful realization,' continued Larter, lighting up his last cigarette and fanning his spent match absently.

Miss Fairchild closed her book and with it the whole subject of Adolphe and his distressing career.

'That sort of reason doesn't make sense,' she said.

The girl's obtuseness worried Kitty who knew that she was by no means stupid. Perhaps she simply had other things on her mind, she thought. Perhaps she finds me dull, tiresome. Yet she is in no way antagonistic. She is even quite pleasant, in a detached sort of manner.

'That is not quite the point,' she replied. 'Romantics would claim greater knowledge of the world, greater understanding of imponderables, greater power of feeling. They would claim greater vulnerability, greater loyalty, greater passion. They might be right or wrong. We are dealing with a work of fiction, and I simply want to make the point that in this period fiction, indeed all creative endeavour, becomes permeated with the author's own autobiography. And yet I think it is important to treat only the finished work – whether it is music or painting or, as in this case, a novel – within the

130

terms of those disciplines. Does *Adolphe* succeed or fail as a novel?'

'Oh, it succeeds,' Larter conceded. 'As an essay in alienation there is nothing like it until Camus.'

'And as a novel there is nothing like it ever again,' said Kitty. 'I am sorry to be so pedantic about words, but the potency of this particular story comes from the juxtaposition of extremely dry language and extremely heated, almost uncontrollable sentiments. If it were overstated, I think I should share Jane's reaction. But there is a feeling that it is almost kept under lock and key, that even if the despair is total, the control remains. This is very elegant, very important. It is also atypical. That is why I chose it. Its early date – 1806 – makes it useful as a yardstick for the shift in consciousness between the eighteenth and the nineteenth centuries. Just think, Napoleon had crowned himself Emperor only two years previously. Some people thought they were living in a new age. Others, more astute, recognized it as a mere interim.'

She paused, seeing their interest suddenly withdrawn. 'Are there any questions?' she asked. 'Yes, what is it, John?' For Larter had quite unceremoniously left the room, only to return, a few seconds later, with a bottle of white wine and four mugs abstracted from the students' canteen.

Mills cleared his throat. 'We wanted to say thank you, Miss Maule. We have enjoyed these sessions very much indeed. And we look forward to your lecture.'

'Hear, hear,' echoed Larter, getting busy with the bottle, while Miss Fairchild reached under the table and produced a tin of biscuits.

'Why, Jane,' said Kitty in astonishment. 'This is really very kind. It is kind of you all,' she corrected herself, for the idea had obviously come from Larter and Mills. Yet the fact that Miss Fairchild had lent herself to the

131

occasion, that she had shown a sign of solidarity, that she had, not to put too fine a point on it, actually joined in, seemed to her immensely encouraging.

The wine, which Larter had concealed in a small sink on the landing, was agreeably chilled, and the biscuits, which Kitty had assumed to be the creation of Miss Fairchild's own hands, turned out to be ordinary digestives, but very welcome, none the less. Kitty felt extremely fond of them, although the afternoon seemed to her not to have been a success. Perhaps *Adolphe* was the wrong book, she thought, although she had previously been convinced that it was the right one. Perhaps they should have had something easier. Berlioz's *Memoirs*, for example.

'You might do a little extra reading, now that you have no more classes,' she said. 'I would recommend Berlioz's *Memoirs*.'

'Oh, terrific stuff,' agreed Larter. 'You haven't got a fag, have you, Kitty? I mean Miss Maule? I've run out.'

'Will you be staying on here?' asked Mills. 'I shall have to say goodbye to everyone at the end of the summer and go back to my own job. But I'd like to know where I could get in touch with you again.'

'I expect I shall be here,' said Kitty, who did not know anything of the sort and indeed did not care to think about the future in those terms.

'We ought to have a reunion in about five or ten years' time,' said Larter, helping himself to another of Kitty's cigarettes and stowing it away in his empty packet. 'On the steps of St Paul's. Carrying a copy of *Adolphe* so that we recognize each other.' He brandished the bottle and tried to refill Mills's mug. 'Come on, you old sot, we know you get drunk every night. Jane?'

Miss Fairchild, who had drunk the wine steadily, as though it were milk, held out her mug. Her cheeks were very faintly flushed, and the hair clung to her damp temples. Holding the bottle in an uncertain hand, Larter looked at her hopelessly. She saw his naked glance, as did the others, changed her mind and shook her head, her eyes lowered, her mouth slightly open. There was a brief silence. After a second or two, Miss Fairchild reached out a delicate hand, took a digestive biscuit, and bit into it with her small even teeth.

Kitty drew a deep breath. *Merde, alors*, she thought. Larter must be protected from this. 'If you'd like to come and see me tomorrow, John,' she said, 'I will give you a bibliography and you can have it photocopied for the others.' She rose and raised her mug. 'To you all,' she said. 'And thank you.'

I handled that badly, she thought, but she was too glad to escape from the room, and the smells of smoke and wine, and the joyless reflections set up by *Adolphe* to devote much time to worrying about what she should have done. She craved the garden, deemed suitable for off-duty thinkers by the kindly manufacturer who had donated the land to the university for this purpose. There paths criss-crossed under the trees now heavy with the leaves of summer, and it was pleasant to walk and meet one's colleagues out of school but still within greeting distance. Kitty hurried down the passage to Pauline's office and found her alone with large sheets of timetable for next year's lectures spread out on the floor beside her.

'Come and have tea,' urged Kitty. 'I feel like strolling in the garden like an ordinary human being. I feel like getting *Adolphe* out of my system. Pauline, I don't think I'm any good at this kind of work.'

'Oh, come on, Kitty, no self-searching, I beg. The Romantics are having a bad effect on you. Can you see my bag?'

'Under the first-year timetable. And frankly, Pauline,

133

that skirt is much too heavy for this weather. How is your mother?'

'Oh, mother's all right,' said Pauline, passing a large, worn powder puff over her otherwise unornamented features. 'The dog gives rise to a certain anxiety, though. You are right about this skirt, of course.'

'I should put it away if I were you. Or get rid of it. Do you think *Adolphe* an accurate reflection of male thinking? On the subject of love, I mean.'

'The trouble is that if I get rid of this skirt I can't wear the jacket and it was frightfully expensive. Cheltenham's best. I think *Adolphe* is a remarkable novel but I doubt if the author is a representative case. And if you are worried about your lecture, kindly do not ruin my tea by worrying out loud. Keep it to yourself and beat the system.'

'Which system.'

'The Romantic Tradition, of course,' said Pauline, who was not her mother's daughter for nothing. At the door she paused and looked back at Kitty who was deep in thought. 'You are very flushed, Kitty. I hope you are not upset. Redmile thinks highly of you, as you well know.'

'If I am flushed, it is because I have been drinking. If I were to think of my work, I should be pale with anxiety. There seems to be no peace around here, all of a sudden. Here you are planning next year, and where am I? Where shall I be?'

'I'm not allowed to tell you,' said Pauline, with a broad grin. 'And I want my tea, please. Look sharp, Kitty. What is the matter with you today?'

'That is the sort of handbag designated as sensible, Pauline. I should get rid of that too, if I were you, while you are about it. I am buying tea today. Eat as much as you like.'

'I shall eat as much as I can,' agreed Pauline, striding

134

on ahead, her sensible handbag banging against her calves. She was glad that she would see Kitty again next year. Kitty, for her part, was weak with relief. I have been working too hard, she thought. I am taking everything too seriously. I shall come back next year and work in a reasonable manner, like Pauline. And I can get through the lecture. I shall have to, since that is what I am going to be paid to do.

With Pauline she took one of the paths leading across the garden to the Senior Common Room. 'You are always so well-dressed, Kitty,' said Pauline.

Kitty reflected. 'Déclassée women like myself frequently are,' she remarked. She looked up and saw two figures coming towards them. 'There is Professor Redmile,' she said in a casual voice, although her heart had begun to beat uncomfortably.

And as Professor Redmile and Maurice drew near, they all raised hands in a mild gesture, smiled, and moved on.

T W E L V E

Kitty Maule, her expression absent, her eyes apparently dazzled by the reflection of the sun on the round rim of a small silver bowl containing rocky pieces of a sweetmeat fabricated by her grandfather, stood very still on a sheet in the middle of her grandparents' sitting room. A bolt of raw silk, the colour of honey, had been breached and now hung about her, firmly tacked. Louise, her expression equally absent, stood with a yardstick in one hand and a cigarette in the other. Vadim his lips pursed, his fingers stroking his jaw, nodded from time to time.

For Kitty, this rite of passage, which she found tiring, uncomfortable, and inappropriate, was nevertheless an essential preliminary to any important occasion. It had been thus all her life: before going to a party, or to her relations in France, or on her birthday, she had had a dress made for her by Louise. The ritual was so familiar as to be unnoticeable: the silent consultation, the gravity of expression, the lengthy fingering of the material, the draping, the pinning, the minute adjustments to a shoulder seam, to the hang of a skirt, to a sleeve, tiny pinchings at the back of the waist, the weighting of the hem. There was never any discussion over the design and colour of these garments, for Louise had always been dictatorial in her professional life. She knew better than anyone else what would be suitable for a particular

136

occasion. She, the product of the rue Saint-Denis and Percy Street, was on more intimate terms with the rituals of society than her many clients, at home with the requirements of royal garden parties, wedding receptions, Glyndebourne, the south of France, Scotland. She had not, it was true, yet designed any clothes suitable for someone giving a talk but she did not doubt that she would be equal to the task. She saw that this might be the last dress she would ever make, and although her eyes were no longer good, although her fingers were getting stiff, although she could no longer kneel, she knew that she would in fact kneel, and pin, and measure, and that the honey-coloured silk, which had been wrapped in black tissue paper since the death of Marie-Thérèse, for whom it had been destined, would finally be made into a dress not only in keeping with her own professional career, now vanished, now hardly remembered, but which would tip the scales in favour of her grand-daughter's future. What that future could be, Louise had little idea. It seemed to her absurd that an event so far outside her own experience that she could not even imagine it – some sort of formal occasion, she gathered, at Thérèse's place of work – should preoccupy her grand-daughter so or indeed have anything to do with their shared life at all. And yet she knew that however outlandish Kitty's activities might seem, she must be there in the form of a guide, of designer; whatever happened to Kitty, Louise would see to it that she was, on this occasion at least, perfectly dressed.

The design that Louise had in mind, a plain shift with long sleeves, was undeniably elegant but seemed to Kitty too fashionable, too positive a statement, too glamorous. There had been a slight argument about this, which was unprecedented, for Louise always knew best and was never questioned, but Kitty had been adamant. 'I need room to move in,' she had said. 'I need a fuller

137

skirt. I need pockets. Is there enough material for a jacket? Maman Louise, don't look at me like that. It will be beautiful, I know, but I can't look too expensive.' She meant, I can't look too old-fashioned, too obvious. She thought of Pauline, indifferent to her baggy skirt, and of how much easier she was to be with than Caroline with her fearless colours and cunning arrangements. She thought, what will Maurice like? Certainly not something tight and straight, like something worn by a model. For myself, I think the material is too elaborate, too noticeable. And yet I need a dress suitable for a formal dinner. Oh, I don't know. I am uneasy about this. 'Maman Louise,' she had said, 'give me some of your pleats.' Louise had been famous for her pleats. There had been a further consultation with Vadim. '*Elle a peut-être raison*,' he had said, anxious to save her time, for he saw that she was not really up to so great an effort. '*Une petite robe avec une jupe plissée. Ligne évasée. Avec un veston. Très décontracté. Tu vois le genre?*' Louise had been unwilling. '*Le tissu est trop important*,' she had murmured, and then she had seen the look in Kitty's eyes, and for the first time in her life she had allowed the girl to have her own way, and the dress had been cut, and pinned, and sewn. And after this fitting it would be finished and she would never see it again. None of these thoughts had shown on her face, which was expressionless. But she had sat up late into the night, too late, perhaps, and the result would be something of which she could be proud.

It had been agreed that Kitty would stay until the dress was finished, which would mean from Saturday to Monday night, when it would be passed in review and given the final seal of approval. This in turn meant that she had a great deal of time on her hands, for both Louise and Vadim were totally absorbed and there was apparently nothing she could say to them. They had retreated into their former lives, were preoccupied with the perfecting of the dress, spoke to each other briefly, like conspirators, like accomplices. Kitty again, as on so many other occasions, tried hard to reconcile the life she lived with them and for them, with the life she lived outside. She had many fears and one great hope and the hope was finally greater than the fears. But the hope, she knew, meant the end of Thérèse and the beginning of Kitty, and the thought of the dress that she would carry away and the occasions on which she would wear it afflicted her with alternate moments of sadness and of joy. The sight of her grandmother kneeling before her to straighten the hem of the dress, the anxiety on her grandfather's face, and that awful moment when Louise had been unable to rise to her feet again and had put out an arm behind her, for Vadim, and the breathlessness that had ensued from the effort of getting her upright: that moment when they had both clung to Louise and lowered her into her chair and had hovered over her until she had recovered and waved them away, affected Kitty like an illness whenever she thought of it. After the incident she had sat quietly in a corner, watching them; then she had gone into the kitchen and made them all a cup of strong coffee, and it was only when Louise had replaced her cup, and had taken a deep breath, and had even eaten a piece of Vadim's dusty fudge, leaving a trail of powdered sugar on her dress, and had snapped her fingers at Vadim and said, 'A toi, maintenant. Débarrasse et aide-moi,' and he had beamed and taken away the tray, and she had started on the hand-sewing of the seams, that Kitty let out her breath, and, feeling suddenly in need of air, had announced that she would be in the garden if they needed her.

But in fact she had been too restless to sit for long and had taken an unremarkable walk in small streets ablaze with summer flowers, and had allowed herself to think of the extraordinary treat ahead of her which, far more than the lecture, would determine her future. She had been at home two Sundays ago, putting the final page into her typewriter, when Maurice had called, quite unannounced. It was the first time she had seen him alone since her return from France and she had been overjoyed. While she made him tea he had sat in her chair and looked through her material. 'This is really very good, Kitty,' he had said. 'You ought to celebrate.' He had looked happy, at ease, and far more relaxed than she ever could, and she longed to put her hand inside his collar and fondle his neck, but she knew she must not. As she was thinking this, he had, amazingly, put out his hand and taken hers. 'It's going to be a good summer, isn't it?' he had said. She had not known what to make of this, but instinct had told her that he meant it for them both. She took his hand between both of hers and said, 'Will you help me to celebrate? Will you come to dinner?' He had laughed and replied, 'No, my darling, you must come to me. I will give a dinner party for you after your lecture. Or perhaps it would be better on the Saturday? What do you think, Kitty? Kitty, why are you looking at me like that? After all, I've had enough meals here.' And he had laughed again and kissed her, lightly, on the cheek.

After that, they had sat together on the sofa and planned the dinner.

'But what about the cooking?' she had asked.

'Oh Ma will lend me Manuela if I ask nicely. Or I'll get somebody else. Don't worry about the cooking. Worry about the guests, Kitty. Whom shall we have? The Redmiles, obviously.'

She pondered. 'The Roger Frys?' she asked. He had cast up his eyes and shuddered elaborately.

'If you must,' he had said. 'If you absolutely must.'

'He does come to your lectures,' she reminded him.

'And she, I suspect, is in love with you.'

He laughed at that, and said, 'All right, but you'll have to keep them amused.'

'Of course,' she had agreed. 'We don't need anybody else, do we? Six is enough, isn't it?'

He had lost interest and had strolled to the window. Hands on hips, he had said, 'Who is that extraordinary woman with the orange hair and the very high heels?' She joined him at the window. 'Oh, Caroline. Caroline Costigan. She lives next door.' Where could Caroline be going on a Sunday? Had she perhaps encountered the man whose name began with J? In the entertainment business? Kitty was so filled with goodwill that she hoped it could be true, and resolved to invite Caroline to supper that evening. For the moment she loved everyone. Voluptuously, she returned to the subject of the dinner party. 'Six will be enough, won't it?' she had asked. 'Six what?' he had said. He was lost in thought, miles away, his arms on the sill. 'Six *guests*,' she had laughed. He had turned round to her, his mild distancing smile back in place. 'Six? Oh, no, I think eight is a better number. I'll think of two others.' His earlier enthusiasm appeared to have waned.

But the promise of a dinner party had been the focus of Kitty's thoughts ever since that day, and the prospect of the lecture had paled into insignificance by the side of it. She imagined that the dinner would be a formal occasion, and wondered, endlessly, if the honey-coloured dress would be adequate. Indeed, she spent most of her evenings, in Old Church Street, worrying about this, and had invoked Caroline's advice on the matter. One evening Caroline had materialized in her doorway when she heard Kitty's steps on the stairs, a voice behind her announcing, 'And now we go over to our friends in Ambridge, where Sid Perks finds he has a problem on his hands,' and had followed Kitty into her

141

flat. Caroline was of the opinion that Kitty looked too austere, that she need touches of colour, and had kindly offered to lend her some jewellery. 'The thing is, Kitty, that your clothes are very well cut, but they need dressing up a bit. You can afford to make more of an impact.' Caroline had then looked through Kitty's wardrobe, draping garments appreciatively against herself or laying them on the bed. As she shook her head slowly over what she saw, Kitty resolved to wear the new dress anyway. Lady Redmile and the Roger Fry Professor's wife, whose unfortunate name was Wendy, would hardly be likely to wear anything more elaborate. She said as much to Caroline, who then had to be invited to stay for supper. 'True,' Caroline agreed. 'And you can slip off the jacket. That way you don't need to worry about a coat. And I will lend you my gold chains.' Kitty thanked her. Caroline sighed elaborately. 'You are lucky, Kitty. I wish someone would invite me out.' 'No luck with the entertainment man?' asked Kitty. 'Not yet, but I went back to her last week, and she's quite definite that I'll be out of here by the end of the year and into something else.' These evenings usually ended far too late, but they had become a bit of an institution. Caroline was as bizarrely attractive as ever, but Kitty, looking at her, and noticing for the first time a slight fattiness on the underside of her jaw, prayed to those indeterminate forces of which she was intermittently aware, 'Don't let her wait too long.'

The unprecedentedly fine weather, the dry sunny evenings, made Kitty long to dispense with all distracting company and to sit or walk alone, thus able better to concentrate on her extraordinary fortune. As it was, she was confined to a dusty calculating world of clothes strewn all over the bed, or condemned to stand in her petticoat in her grandmother's flat, a lay figure, unwilling to lend herself to the business of her own adornment, which, she felt, should be accomplished by herself, alone, in secret. She looked forward to that Saturday evening when, in decent obscurity, and with no accompanying remarks, no rectification of the shoulder seams, no strictly professional appraisal, she would prepare herself and sit quietly at the window, savouring the enormous and unbearable pleasure of waiting for the taxi that would take her to Maurice. She would have liked to shut her door to Caroline whose intention, she knew, was to oversee every stage of the ritual, from the vantage point of a greater experience of the world. But Kitty also knew that she had her own ritual to follow, and that it was fraught with superstition, that if she did not obey her own imperatives, something would be wrong and the evening would be ill-omened. She could not have said what this ritual was, but she perceived that it was something to do with acknowledgment of the luck that had come to her, that in fact her earlier bewildered searchings and dreads had been neutralized, sanctioned, that she was no longer a petitioner, that plans had been made in which she had a part. For this supreme leniency on the part of fate she did not know what or whom to thank, but made a polite obeisance in the direction of what she now regarded as Providence, and for this, she needed to be alone.

As she sat in the garden of her grandparents' house, she was aware that the time had come to say goodbye to those who had been with her on the first half of her journey, and that she must now prepare to live a different sort of life. No more clairvoyants, no more waiting in hotel rooms, no more glum acceptance of Caroline's advice. From now on she would be more definite, more admirable, she thought. She would eat reasonable meals, she would not panic before her lecture, she would deal sensibly with everyone, but would not allow anyone to dominate her. She was saying goodbye to her very pliancy, the quality that had kept her, like her mother, a girl for far too long. And I am thirty she said to herself. I am already thirty. It is time.

For two days she sat in the garden or walked about the streets, and she would remember those two days as a curious interval, when all things seemed possible, an almost mystical time of promise and anticipated fulfilment. The hours of the day were uniform in their bright silent intensity, and the sun did not appear to move. There was a suspension of appetite and of all agitation, replaced by an extraordinary concentration of the faculties, a stillness, something strange and new. It was as if some genuine metamorphosis were taking place, yet she did not know what it was.

From time to time she returned to the dusky interior of the house, to the smells of coffee and Vadim's plum brandy, to the hushed atmosphere that always accompanied Louise's concentration on her task. Kitty cleared away the plates from which snacks had been eaten hastily, abstractedly; a crust of bread already hardening in the heat, a rind of sausage or cheese, the peel of a fruit, empty mustard glasses containing the dregs of wine. She recorked the bottle and put it away, then silently emptied the ashtray and replaced it at her grandmother's elbow. The heavy dull yellow silk lay in a pool in her grandmother's lap, although the jacket was finished, had been pressed by Vadim, and was now displayed on the dressmaker's dummy in the spare room, where it strained over the descending swan-like bosom and flared over the unindented hips. But the dress, the dress! Sometimes it seemed to Kitty as though it would never be finished, as if the minute stitches would go on for ever, as if there were always another seam, another pleat, as if it might have to be dismantled and started again. And she did not think she could bear to sit either in the silent room or in the silent garden much longer. For now impatience, like a deeper than normal heartbeat, was beginning to make itself felt in her, and she wanted to get through the intervening time between this moment and that Saturday, to abolish the journeys and the fitting and the lecture and all the meals she would have to eat between now and then, and to find herself sitting at her window, in her final moment of waiting, before the beautiful evening was to begin.

At the end, the tension in the sitting room was too much for her. Louise seemed not to have moved from her chair for two days. Kitty carried out with her, into the sunshine, an image of Louise, in her dusty black dress, with a powdering of sugar on the breast, her face impassive, her swollen feet propped on a footstool, stitching with rapid unhesitating strokes. Vadim moving silently around her, his expression watchful, almost severe. The room indifferent to the splendour outside, aromatic and enclosed. In the garden Kitty sat and waited for the hours to pass. It stayed light until very late and she had no idea of the time. Finally, on the Monday, as she was sitting, she heard the window above her open, and turning, saw her grandfather's head emerge, and heard him say, '*Ça y est. Viens, Thérèse.*'

Standing on a sheet in the middle of the floor, she submitted while Louise dropped the dress over her head, while Vadim turned her round and secured it, while Louise then lifted the dress on the shoulders and let it settle. She stood quite still as Louise stepped back, lit a cigarette, and contemplated her handiwork. She stood until the cigarette was smoked, the inspection finished. Not a word was exchanged. Then Louise turned to Vadim and nodded to him. His face broke into his great smile and he kissed her cheek. Then Kitty was allowed to see herself in the glass. The dress was exquisite, so light, so easy, with the famous pleats breaking about the knees, and the long graceful jacket. I cannot possibly

145

wear any of Caroline's jewellery with this, thought Kitty. I shall have to put it on to save her feelings and keep it in my bag for the rest of the evening. I must remember to put it on when I get back to Old Church Street in case she is still up and about. Then she turned to her grandmother who motioned her to walk up and down, and then when she was back on the sheet and her grandmother seated, she said, 'It is perfect.' She took the dress off and gave it to Vadim who packed it carefully in layers of tissue paper and put it into a bag. As if I were a customer, thought Kitty, with a pang. She knelt by the side of her grandmother's chair, longing to lay her head on the worn velvet of the arm. When she could speak, she said, 'Thank you.' Louise looked at her, with no apparent emotion, even a certain distant gravity. Then she reached out her hand, pinched Kitty's chin and said, 'Vas-y, ma fille.'

They all had a cup of coffee together, and it was so late, and they were so tired, that they had little to say to each other. Kitty wanted to see them both into bed, but they never would allow that. With a sigh, she realized that she must leave them, that the long day had finally come to an end, that the time of contemplation was behind her and the time of action about to be inaugurated. She was irritated by this solemn thought and anxious to be done with it for it had no place in her new life, in which everything was possible. So she collected the cups quite briskly and marched into the kitchen and put it to rights, and tried to break the mood that had intensified around them. She gathered up her things and kissed them both goodnight, and went out into the evening air, breathing deeply. As she turned to give them a last wave, as she always did, she saw their two faces at the window, white masks that dwindled as she walked backwards down the hill, still waving.

146

T H I R T E E N

Kitty, waving goodbye at the gate, saw Pauline Bentley stow her mother carefully into the car. She had offered to stay at home and mind the dog while Pauline undertook the one annual outing to which Mrs Bentley remained faithful, despite her loathing of being transported anywhere by any means she could not control. They were going to a fête at a large house in an adjoining village; Mrs Bentley had known the previous owners and considered it her duty as an upholder of the old regime to support the nurses' charity to which the proceeds would go, although she voiced her loud disapproval every time someone shook a collecting box under her nose. They were, Mrs Bentley had told Kitty, to sit in the rose garden, which she had always admired, talk to one or two people, have a cup of tea, and come home.

Kitty, lingering by the gate, saw them in her mind's eye, as if admitted to a larger gathering or assembly than she had ever enjoyed, conversing with people of greater breadth and ease. What were they wearing, she wondered? What would be suitable? Mrs Bentley had gone off in her sandals, with her tin in the pocket of her usual cardigan; Pauline had worn an unimpressive pair of trousers. She herself would have tried harder, she thought.

But Pauline, steering her mother over tussocks of bleached grass, and quite unaware of Kitty's disapproval, felt that she was trying quite hard enough, particularly as her mother had forgotten where she was and was demanding reassurance in her usual carrying tones.

'I can't remember what I am doing here,' said Mrs Bentley, stopping dead and shading her sightless eyes, 'although I dare say it makes a change. But what sort of change is it making, my dear? Are you smuggling me into an old folks' home? Will you abandon me in the middle of this field, or whatever it is? More to the point, have I got time for a smoke?'

'You know perfectly well, Mother, that this is the most splendid treat and that you are going to enjoy every minute of it.'

'Then when is it going to start?' asked Mrs Bentley with interest.

'The moment we get out of this apology for a car park and into the main garden. I thought we might sit by the roses and inhale.'

'Ah,' said Mrs Bentley, 'I remember. The Gretton's place. Open Day, and people I have never met telling me how marvellous I am looking. Shall we have tea?'

'It is only three-fifteen, Mother.'

'I see nothing wrong with that.'

'If I could remember where I put the car, we can do whatever you like,' said Pauline, looking over her shoulder.

'I do wish your friend could have joined us. It can't be much fun for her with just the dog for company. Although he appreciates it, of course.'

But Kitty was at that moment genuinely lost in the Romantic Tradition and the dog observed a suitable silence.

'She is putting the final touches to her lecture, Mother,' said Pauline, quite accurately. 'It is this coming

Tuesday, you know. We shall tell her all about the fête when we get home.'

'Why are you speaking so slowly, Pauline? Is anything wrong?'

'Why should anything be wrong?' asked Pauline, who had just caught sight of Maurice Bishop striding along with an unaccustomed air of elation about him. 'Let us go along here,' she added, taking her mother by the elbow, but she was forestalled, and it would have been too impolite to have turned away at this stage.

'Mother,' she said. 'Here is Maurice Bishop.'

'Why, Maurice,' cried Mrs Bentley. 'How delightful! Is your mother with you?'

Pauline and Maurice gazed steadily and warningly into each other's eyes. 'How are you, Mrs Bentley?' said Maurice. 'You are looking simply splendid. Can I get you some tea?'

'Thank you so ... What *is* it, Pauline? Are you ill?'

'You will forgive us, won't you?' said Pauline. 'It is getting so crowded that I think we will just stroll round the rose garden and then go home for tea,' and nodding her head twice in farewell, she grasped her mother by the arm and directed her none too gently to the rose garden, where they sat for ten minutes, Mrs Bentley expostulating between drags on a half-dead cigarette, and Pauline rather silent.

'You were quite overbearing, Pauline. I should have liked to talk to Maurice. After all, I have known him since he was a boy. Has he got over that girl yet?'

'I really couldn't say, Mother.'

A shred of flaming tobacco fell on to Mrs Bentley's skirt and was brushed off by Pauline as a matter of course. An intriguing thought struck Mrs Bentley.

'Are you in love with him, Pauline? I should quite understand it if you were. But that is no excuse for behaving as you did. A little finesse, my dear. There is

149

no point in wearing your heart on your sleeve.'

'In fact,' said Pauline, 'I rather dislike him. I always have, now that I come to think of it. Shall we go home and surprise Kitty? She is our guest, after all.'

In the car Mrs Bentley expressed a desire to attend Kitty's lecture but was told by Pauline that the journey would tire her too much.

'But I am so fond of her. Tell me, Pauline, what does she look like?'

Pauline thought. 'She looks very pretty when she is animated and rather plain when she is not.'

Mrs Bentley nodded. '*Journalière*, that used to be called. What else?'

'She is very well-dressed, almost too well-dressed. Oh, I suppose she is quite attractive. They think highly of her in the Department.'

'She has such a pretty voice,' said Mrs Bentley. 'Such very precise English. You rarely hear such good enunciation these days. It comes from her being a foreigner, of course.'

'Oh, really, Mother. She was born in London. Although I agree that she gives the impression of someone not quite at home here. Trying to learn the rules, as it were.'

'I should call her well-bred, and that says it all. The natives, after all, don't have to bother.'

There were many reasons why Pauline did not want to pursue the subject of Kitty, who, she felt, must be having a perfectly ghastly weekend, and so she diverted her mother from this particular topic of conversation by trying to persuade her to give up smoking, as she did, in the line of duty, at least once a week.

'You nearly set fire to yourself this afternoon.'

'I didn't even notice,' said Mrs Bentley absently. 'But what a spectacular way to go. It might even be on the wireless.'

'I should have bought a cake at one of those stalls,' mused Pauline. 'Kitty will be starving to death.'

But Kitty had had quite a pleasant dreamy afternoon in the little garden, reading her lecture superstitiously, although she knew it was finished, and even rather good. She walked down to the local shop and bought a packet of waxen tea cakes and toasted them and put the kettle on and so a second tea was ready when Pauline and Mrs Bentley got home – the least she could do, Kitty felt, for Pauline had been so kind with her invitations, and was prepared to drive Kitty to the station whenever she decided to leave. Kitty was anxious now to get back to London and the intense absorbing ritual she had devised for herself and which now afflicted her with shivers of anticipation. So that when she asked Mrs Bentley if she would excuse her shortly after tea, explaining that she still had more work to do, although she had not, and had patted the still comatose dog, and met Pauline's eyes fixed on her in some sort of speculation, she felt the visit had reached a quite natural conclusion. She kissed Mrs Bentley, who appeared a little surprised, but pleased by the attention. 'I wish you all good fortune on Tuesday, my dear,' said Mrs Bentley in her usual loud conversational tones. 'Remember to aim your voice at the back of the room. And try not to look at anyone in particular. They will begin to wonder if you are sending out secret messages and then you will wonder what you have done to make them so uneasy, and then you will lose your nerve.' It was not a cheerful piece of advice, but Kitty felt it was a useful one. I must remember not to look at Maurice, she thought.

She was rather silent in the car, thinking of the various ordeals of the week to come. Her lecture was in the evening and Professor Redmile had invited her to drink a glass of sherry beforehand – 'although I am sure you will not need Dutch courage, Miss Maule. We know

151

the quality of your material. Great stuff. Great stuff.'
The occasion, thought Kitty, would be even more taxing
than the lecture itself, particularly as there would be
several people there and whenever this occurred Professor Redmile tended to confide in them details of the
revised estimates for the New Building. Glazed with
boredom, his guests invariably drank too much, and
Kitty had visions of them falling asleep during the
lecture, rending the air with their snores and having to
be elbowed awake when it was all over. For the lecture
itself she could trust herself to her typescript and
Louise's dress; if I can keep my nerve, I shall be quite
effective. Whatever Mrs Bentley says, I must remember
not to shout. That is not the dress for shouting in. And I
must get plenty of sleep between now and Saturday.

London was silent in the heat and although the
weather was so exceptionally fine the streets seemed to
be deserted. She reached the flat in an anxious though
somnolent state which surprised her; she put it down to
the effects of so much concentration and to Mrs
Bentley's curiously jarring command not to look at
anyone while she was lecturing. She had imagined
herself communing eagerly with her audience, and had
seen them responding to her with equal eagerness; she
had envisaged the sort of open exchange that always
seemed to elude her. And now, she realized, it was to be
yet another solo performance of high strain. She sighed,
and let herself into the flat.

Through the wall there came the sound of a robust
and actorish voice describing sheep-stealing in
Elizabethan England. Within minutes, Caroline
knocked on the door and was revealed to Kitty's gaze in
a violet cotton print dress, violet sandals, and violet
eye-shadow to match. She had evidently spent the entire
day refurbishing herself, for her hair and nails were
immaculate. 'Thank God you're home,' she said. 'I've

been dying of boredom.' She advanced into Kitty's flat, leaving the sheep-stealing recital behind her. 'It must have been marvellous in the country. You are lucky, Kitty. Nobody ever asks me out now.'

'But all your friends ... ' Kitty began.

'Well, now that I'm divorced they don't want to know me. You know how it is with a woman on her own. The wives close ranks. A woman on her own is a threat, Kitty.'

Kitty, who could not see Caroline as a threat, said nothing. Then, realizing that Caroline meant to stay for the rest of the evening, she calculated how many eggs she had left. 'You'll have a snack with me, won't you?' she said pleasantly. And even more pleasantly, 'Why don't you switch that thing off and leave it off for a bit? You cannot, by the remotest stretch of the imagination, be interested in Elizabethan sheep.'

Caroline laughed, drifted off, then drifted back again, displacing a small cloud of scent. 'Actually, I don't want anything to eat. It's too hot. Why don't you show me what you're going to wear for your lecture? I haven't seen your dress yet.' Kitty, seeing her face rosy and childlike with anticipation, went obediently to the bedroom to prepare herself. The dress was as good as ever, but Kitty did not like what she saw. I am strained, she thought; this waiting is telling on me. And I am tired of the company of women. If only I could see Maurice. If only he were here instead of Caroline. Why does he not come to me? Do I have to give a lecture to engage his attention? Must I avoid his eyes in the hall at the very moment when I need to read some message in them? Why does he keep me waiting so long?

'Very nice,' said Caroline, in a dubious sort of voice. 'But don't you think you ought to liven it up a bit? I think if you wore my chains and a vivid scarf ... Actually it's your face that needs dressing up a bit, if you don't mind my saying so, Kitty. Just stay there. I'll be back in a minute.'

When she returned, it was with an armoury of bottles and jars and brushes, and a pair of sandals with very high heels. Instructing Kitty to try them for size, she darted into the bathroom for a towel, and draping it around Kitty's shoulders, proceeded to transform her, humming with pleasure as she did so. I must let her get on with this, thought Kitty, suppressing a yawn; it has clearly saved her evening. Although it is rather ruining mine.

Her face, which Caroline demonstrated to her with pride, was enlivened with many colours: green on the eyelids, a curious brick pink on the cheeks and mouth. She looked, in fact, like a bad facsimile of Caroline. When she had been draped in the chains and scarves, she saw, with interest, that she resembled a prostitute she had once seen emerging from the George-Cinq. A cynical, capable, and utterly French other self had emerged, and this self was not the sort of woman who gave lectures or aspired to the unity of a simple life or desired to align herself with the beliefs and customs of the established majority. This startling face held promises of great assurance, of sophistication; this was a face that belonged to a woman who knew how to please. Caroline was delighted with it. 'The thing is, Kitty, that you sometimes look a bit depressed, if you don't mind my saying so. As if you've ... I don't know, been stood up, or something. In fact, you want to take the initiative a bit more. Nothing's going to happen if you just sit in this flat.' She sighed. 'I should know.' She looked so tragic that Kitty went to put the kettle on. Changing out of her dress, but with her face still adorned, she wondered how she could get rid of Caroline at a reasonable hour, remove all traces of her ministrations, and get a good night's sleep.

154

It was, they agreed, an incredible summer. It was also a particularly poignant evening, and after they had eaten their scrambled eggs, Kitty suggested a walk by the river. But Caroline declined, and seemed to want to talk about people whom Kitty did not know, people who had been in Caroline's 'set', as she called it, when her fortunes had been at their highest. Kitty listened politely, her mind absent. I shall see him the day after tomorrow, she thought. And then after that I can telephone him about Saturday, to see if there's anything he wants me to do. It seems absurd to feel so shy of him, but I am only like this when we are apart. Paris seems such a long time ago. If only we could go back there, this summer. In the car, this time. I should like him to show me France. There is nothing I can show him; he cannot be expected to be interested in what I know. I wish Caroline would go. I am longing to get this stuff off my face.

Caroline, becoming more discontented by the minute, left eventually on a rather mournful trailing note, and within seconds the sound of the late news bulletin was seeping through the wall. Minutes later she knocked at Kitty's door. 'I forgot to wish you luck,' she said. 'But you'll be all right. I'll look in and see how you're getting on.' In which case, thought Kitty, there is every reason for my being out for most of tomorrow. If she tries to do my face again, I may go mad. I shall simply have to sit in the garden. Oh, I am fed up with sitting in gardens by myself. I want it to be different now. I don't want to be alone any more.

She tidied the kitchen, then went into her bedroom, which still showed signs of Caroline's efforts. She smoothed the counterpane, and put the bottles that Caroline had forgotten to take away with her on one side. On an impulse she slipped on the dress again and tried to look at herself dispassionately in the glass. She saw a graceful figure but one that did not seem quite right; it was too formal, perhaps, too self-conscious. It was what Louise would have described as well-groomed, with all that that implies of deliberate presentation. Then she realized what had worried her ever since she had got the dress home and examined herself in her own flat, in her own room. I look as I looked at Jean-Claude's wedding.

He had married a noisy little dark girl called Christiane and Louise had sent Kitty over to represent the family. There had been a very pretty ceremony in the bride's village church and in the afternoon there had been a gigantic meal that had lasted until five o'clock. A rather grandly placed cousin had lent her house and they had all sat down at a long table on the lawn and had drunk champagne with every one of the numerous courses. She was amused and a little wistful, particularly when Jean-Claude, whom she thought had forgotten her, raised his glass to her, the visitor from England, and of course she had had to respond. You next, they chorused, the old greedy aunts, the small philosophical uncles, you next. When you put away those books it will be your turn. Soon, soon. And she had smiled and shaken her head, and they had poured out more champagne.

And when they had finished the enormous meal and when the light was beginning to fade, and a little wind had sprung up, flapping the corners of the damask tablecloth, they had gone into the house and had started to dance, the heavy aunts and shrivelled uncles, Christiane in her white dress, noisier and more vivid than ever, and eventually Jean-Claude had asked her to dance and had held her almost as he had once held her, his breath warm on her hair. But she was a little shy of him now, for he seemed such a reformed character, so smart, so promising, that it was difficult to remember

156

the hotel room with the slice of ham curling up in the greasy paper and the rickety table by the window. For now he was a professional man and a married man; he had a career ahead of him and he was about to take up his abode in a *maison de caractère* which his wife's parents had bought for them in the suburbs. She hardly knew what to say to him and was silent. But when the dance ended, he had kissed her lightly and said, 'You should always wear that colour. Yellow is your colour. And ask me to your wedding soon. I hope you will be as happy as I am today.'

As the evening grew dim, and the aunts and the uncles lingered in chairs around the edges of the room sipping coffee and asking about Louise, Kitty had tried to tell them that she and Vadim were quite well and still devoted, but she knew with a pang how much they had missed coming and how they dared not look forward to another wedding like this – dared not because it no longer seemed possible. The aunts and the uncles had nodded, not needing her words, for they had assessed the situation and the neat graceful girl so different from themselves. They had packed up boxes of petits fours for her to take home, and had given her a bottle of champagne and told her to tell them to drink the bride's health, and they would drink hers. And the evening had ended a little sadly, with great fatigue, and it had turned chill, but as she left in somebody's car, she had heard the sound of the accordion still playing in the empty lighted room.

This memory now came back to her with vivid force and she wondered how she could have mislaid it. Louise and Vadim had nodded over her account of the wedding and had brooded over the photographs that had been sent: many taken of the bride and groom, one of Christiane in her white dress, looking back commandingly over her shoulder, and one of the whole family

157

standing, with glasses upraised, behind the long table with the damask tablecloth. Ah, they breathed. And they had nibbled the petits fours and said, no, they would keep the champagne. For another occasion, they said. And they had all wondered, separately, and silently, when that would be.

But since Kitty had met Maurice she had formed her own idea of what a wedding should be like, and realized that the charming afternoon in France with the heavy aunts and the neat uncles would not be repeated. And uneasy thoughts of suitability had come into her mind; she could not get rid of them. They were the people who remembered her mother (although there had been no means of getting them to that wedding) and one or two of them had shed a tear even after this long time as they thought of her sad death. And Kitty had felt softened and yet ashamed as she watched the tears slipping down the red faces, past the blurred mouths, and watched the thick, ringed fingers smearing the robust make-up with dignified handkerchiefs. Her own wedding she had never dared to think of, unless ... unless she could reproduce that occasion more perfectly, could persuade the same grand cousin to donate the same grand house, to place another long table on the same summer lawn, and so to delight her bridegroom with the strangeness and charm of the occasion that all barriers would be forgotten and national inhibitions would be overcome. But it now seemed to her that she herself had become a different person from the girl she had been on that occasion, that she had been concentrating too long on something that was no longer appropriate to that former time, that she was now less innocent, more strained, more ardent, and that the aunts and the uncles, were they to see her this evening, were they to know how she had passed her Sunday, sitting in a dark little cottage in the middle of England, would have shaken

158

their heads in dismay, would have pursed their lips, would have written to Louise demanding an explanation. It is not her fault, thought Kitty, standing still in her bedroom. It is not her fault at all. It is mine.

For she had embraced what she thought of as her father's tradition, although she had never known him and had no real idea of what he stood for. She had made the young soldier in the faded photograph her image of England just as she had made Maurice her ideal of England. And that image and that ideal had none of the solidity of the red faces and the accordion and artful Christiane with her white veil and her carefully arranged train and the soulful face looking over her shoulder as the village photographer had instructed. And she had schooled herself not to remember Jean-Claude's breath on her hair and his wish for her to be as happy as he was on that day, and had substituted for it an admiration for carelessness, a more powerful because understated charm, and a file of lecture notes which she had had too much time to amass. And as she put the dress away she thought, but I decided all this the day I met him and I cannot go back now, for there is nothing to go back to. I will wait and hope. Beauty for ashes. I must wait and hope. For everyone turns into something else, and I can do it too.

In her cool bed, in the silent night, she was calm and very tired. She thought of her strange weekend and of the even stranger week that lay ahead. There is no power on earth, she thought, that can keep me from what I love. And it is really quite appropriate and even rather amusing that I have to give this lecture, so that I am launched into the life that I shall have to live, and shall learn to live, with Professor Redmile and Pauline and all the others instead of the uncles and the aunts. And there will be no music, no champagne, no dancing, but the world instead, and books, and cathedrals, and I

159

shall learn and shall send them postcards. To show that I have not forgotten them. But I have already left them behind. Their way is not my way. My way is not their way.

And as she drifted into sleep she envisaged a life of very great fullness and happiness, teaching, learning, taking notes, taking note; she saw herself calm, and pleasant, and controlled, and suitable. The landscape of Gloucestershire opened out to her once more, and she saw that Pauline and Mrs Bentley inhabited it perfectly. And she remembered the day she had had tea in the garden of The Manor and saw that it would be perfectly possible to live her life in this mode, if she were to be given the chance. And as her breathing became steadier and she turned on her side to sleep, she felt quite safe in her resolve and her ambition, and the week to come appeared quite possible, and she thought with love and pity of Jean-Claude dancing with his bride and his toast to her in the champagne that had become warm in the sun and his breath on her hair, and at last she slept.

But later that night she burned in fires.

F O U R T E E N

The night had been so extremely disturbing that when she struggled out of the brief sleep that had finally overtaken her and sat up in bed preparing to face a day in which nothing awaited her but yet another revision of her manuscript, Kitty felt suddenly vanquished and in need of help.

The sun was already high and hot and the weather forecast, which she could hear on Caroline's radio, confirmed that it would be another exceptional day; drivers were warned to take care on overheated and melting tarmac. Kitty Maule tried and failed to finish her cup of coffee, ate an apple instead, took a long cool bath and put on an old cotton frock. It was then that she remembered the clairvoyant.

She stood still, arrested, in the middle of the room, her hands clenched in the pockets of her skirt, wondering if she should say anything to Caroline. But then she knew that she must be very silent about this, and, unconsciously, as she turned towards the door, she willed herself to be noiseless and hardly released her breath until she was out of the building.

Despising herself, yet impelled through the streets, she wondered if the woman would be able to see her and was unable to face the possibility that she might not, that she might even be away. But she found the cat still on the windowsill of the small house with the bottle green door and when she rang the bell it was answered immediately by Madame Eva, dressed in a flowered overall, looking mildly through her glasses, with a duster in her hand.

'Hello, dear,' she said. 'Were you wanting a reading?'

Kitty nodded, incapable of speech.

The woman hesitated. 'I was just going out to do me shopping. In this heat you don't feel like doing it later in the day.' She looked at Kitty more sharply. 'Lots of tension round you, isn't there?' She shoved the duster into the pocket of her overall, then beckoned Kitty to come in. 'I'll just make meself a coffee,' she said. 'Go in, dear. You know the way.'

Kitty sank with relief into the soft dirty cushions of the sagging armchair and gazed at the motes of dust she had dislodged as they swirled in the morning sun. Now that she was here she felt no inclination to move for the rest of the day. Her fatigue and her dismay were suddenly in abeyance, although her heart was beating rather strongly, and her hands, she noticed, were trembling. The cat, which had padded in silently behind her took up its place on a small table by the window and yawned from time to time. Madame Eva, treading heavily, came in with a cup of coffee and sat down in a creaking basket chair opposite Kitty. For a moment or two they said nothing, although between sips which she heard rather than saw Kitty was aware that the woman was appraising her.

'You're looking ever so well,' she said finally. 'Been in the country? You're a striking girl,' she added, wiping her mouth with a folded pale green tissue. 'Unusual. Mind you don't undervalue yourself, now.'

Kitty smiled at her with gratitude. I shall get the truth again, she thought. I got it last time. Although I cannot now remember the details.

With her usual sigh, the woman reached into the bag by the side of her chair and produced the crystal ball, which she polished with a large silk handkerchief. She seemed less impassive, more uncomfortable in the heat than she had the last time. Kitty remembered what a strain she had said the work was causing her, and glanced instinctively at the pyramid of hair, which was immaculate. Madame Eva shifted in her chair, then bent forward and cupped her hands round Kitty's and was silent once again.

'You have been thinking about weddings lately,' she said.

Kitty started, looked up, then looked down again as she felt the hands pressing hers more firmly.

'Oh, yes, you've been thinking about weddings. Somewhere in the country?'

Kitty nodded, but said nothing. The woman sighed again and moved about in her chair.

'I see a room with a lot of people. You're there in front of them. I don't know what this means.'

'I do,' murmured Kitty, her eyes half closed now in some kind of drowsy anticipation of what she knew she was going to hear.

'Success,' said the woman suddenly and focused her eyes sharply on Kitty. 'Terrific success. No need to worry.' She removed one hand and wiped her mouth again with the green tissue which she replaced in the pocket of her overall.

'And after?' ventured Kitty in a timid voice.

The woman sighed again. 'You've got a lot of admirers,' she said slowly. 'You're quite surrounded.'

This meant nothing to Kitty, who determined to ignore it.

The woman shifted again, clearly uncomfortable in the heat. 'Did you know you were going to become rather important?' she said. 'There are people around

163

you. You won't be alone. You've been alone rather a lot, haven't you?'

Kitty nodded.

'That's over,' the medium said. 'That's over now. You won't be isolated in the same way again. You'll be very secure, very established.' She bent further over the cupped hands. 'Very respectable,' she added.

Kitty's heart beat more strongly and she looked with gratitude at Madame Eva. She saw that the woman was in some distress from the heat, that moisture had formed on her upper lip, that her heavy body was uneasy in its casing of flowered nylon. Yet the hands that enclosed hers were dry and strong and she was amazed at the firmness of the control they exercised over her, willing her to remain sunk in the dirty armchair, although, quite suddenly, she was ready to leave. She would go back to the flat and make herself a decent breakfast, and clear up properly, and take advantage of the sun and read something sensible. She began to feel ashamed of the impulse that had brought her to this room.

She felt her hands turned over and, glancing down, saw the woman examining the palms.

'You're a little bit psychic yourself,' she said. 'Did you know that?'

'Well, I sometimes get odd feelings that I don't understand. But then everybody does, surely?'

'Yes, to a certain extent.' She hesitated and then let Kitty's hands drop. 'Was there anything you wanted to ask me, dear?'

'You said you saw a wedding,' Kitty said diffidently. 'Will it take place soon?'

The pale green tissue was plied once again. 'Oh yes,' said the medium. 'Definitely a wedding.' She seemed abstracted, sighed again, and plucked another coloured tissue from the box at her side. 'Good luck, dear. All the best. Same terms as before. Your friend all right, is she?'

'I think she gets a bit lonely,' said Kitty, handing over the money.

'I daresay she does. Won't be long now, though. Well, dear, all the best.'

She saw her to the door; the cat bounded out past her and disappeared down the street. They looked after it, admiring its agility in this great heat. At mid morning it was advisable to seek the shade; instinctively Kitty and Madame Eva put up a hand to their eyes.

'Too hot for me,' sighed the woman. 'I don't feel much like going out, to tell you the truth. I'll make do with what I've got.'

'What was it you wanted?' asked Kitty. 'I could get it for you. I rather like this weather.'

Madame Eva looked at her and smiled. 'I only want a loaf,' she said. 'And a couple of tins of sardines. One for me, one for him. And a few tomatoes. I've got all the rest. Are you sure? It would save me going out. Take my purse then, love. No hurry. I'll be in all day.'

Kitty took some money from the purse and put it in her own. She turned into the melting street, hesitated, then went into a café and ordered a substantial breakfast. This she ate with great pleasure, and, feeling invigorated by the food and the heat, left a large tip and determined to do some serious shopping when she got Madame Eva's supplies. She was no longer very much aware of the time for she was going over in her mind the concepts of respectability, success, and a wedding that had been handed out to her, and a general sense of euphoria seemed to have overtaken her, making her feel at one with the summer sunshine and the odd leisure of this interim day.

She did the shopping and made her way back to the medium's house, but when she rang the bell there was no answer. She rang it again, puzzled, for the woman had said she was not going out. She stepped back into

165

the street and scanned the upstairs windows. There was no sound. Then the door of the neighbouring house opened a little and a large calm blonde head appeared, and shortly after it a stocky body dressed in trousers and a bright blue cotton blouse. 'Were you wanting Mrs Cartwright?' asked the neighbour.

'Madame Eva,' Kitty said uncertainly. 'I did some shopping for her.'

'I expect she's popped out for a moment,' said the neighbour, stretching out her hand for the bag. 'I'll take the things, shall I?'

'She said she wasn't going out,' murmured Kitty, handing over the shopping bag.

'Oh, she won't have gone far. You'll probably see her around.' And the door was politely but firmly shut.

Kitty, a little disconcerted, wandered slowly away in the direction of the main street. It seemed to her odd, even disquieting, that Madame Eva, whom she now had to think of as Mrs Cartwright, should have disappeared when she had seemed so perturbed by the thought of going out. As she reached the corner, she looked back, and was heartened to see the medium, with the cat in her arms, just emerging from a small turning opposite her house. She caught sight of Kitty and waved, and Kitty waved back, strangely relieved. And facing each other, walking backwards, each waved until the other was out of sight.

Kitty was amazed to see that it was nearly one o'clock. Suddenly the rest of the day had ceased to be a problem. She bought a newspaper and went back to the café and ate lunch. She scanned her paper and ordered more coffee, waiting until the small crowd had left and gone back to work. There was no sound now but the hiss of the coffee machine, and the tuneless melancholy whistling of the Italian owner. Kitty, seated beside the plate glass window, looked out indulgently at the street, but, finding the people too distracting and her own thoughts too important, dropped her eyes to the table and to the glass vase holding three dark red and rather exhausted carnations and turned them about and lifted the vase to her nose for the sweet and faintly rotten smell and even brushed her face against the thin and infinitely soft petals, wondering at the tightness of the stem and the complexity of the flower. Then, putting the vase down, she lit a cigarette and smiled faintly to see how the time was getting on and that soon she could wander home and make a cup of tea and then it would not be long until the evening, when she really would have to work, and she would be in bed early and the way ahead would be quite simple.

But still she sat, eyeing the carnations, the smoke of her cigarette drifting round her head, until the Italian owner called out, 'Another coffee, signora?' and she started, and nodded, and said, 'And the bill, please', and gave him her newspaper, and taking a deep breath she stubbed out her cigarette and drank her coffee and went out into the street, where people were complaining of the heat, but humorously, as if enjoying the ordeal. As she made her way back to the flat she felt as if she had passed the day in a dream, and indeed something of the dreamlike mood still persisted, even as she looked through her manuscript once more, and shampooed her hair, and stripped her bed and made it up with fresh sheets. The same atmosphere of dream impelled her to sit in the window, and she did not really notice the light diminishing its glare and the shadows lengthening. It was not until eight that she got up and made coffee and ate an apple, and shortly after that went to bed.

She slept heavily and deeply and awoke feeling very calm.

She was out of the house by eleven, and in her yellow dress, with her ordinary face, she felt quite equal to the

167

brilliant day. She travelled alone, and walked with pleasure from the station to the university. She lunched with Pauline and then spent the afternoon in Pauline's room, soothed by her undemanding presence. Pauline kept her eyes firmly on the examination schedules. She did not want any part of this initiation ceremony; she thought that Kitty looked like an obedient child before a party, and although she was moved by Kitty's happy expectancy, she rejected the idea that she might be responsible for any extensive nurturing. She had had enough of that.

'Right,' she said at last, scrubbing her face with her powder puff. 'Let's get it over, then. Redmile, I mean. The rest belongs to history and I take no responsibility for it. Come along, Kitty, look sharp. Your dress is very nice. Are you sure you remember what this is all about? You seem to be in a dream.'

Kitty cleared her throat. 'I am quite ready,' she said.

'Ah, Miss Maule,' exclaimed Professor Redmile. 'And Dr Bentley. How very pleasant. Do come in.' He was good at this sort of thing, they had to acknowledge. He managed to keep up a steady blast of hilarity until the last guest had departed; he went to so many parties that he rarely had to think about what to say, having learnt that remarks of any consequence were out of place on such occasions, particularly as one was quite unable to hear a reply, if one were ever forthcoming. There were quite a few people there: Kitty noticed the Professors of Spanish and German, the Roger Fry Professor, looking hot and glum, and his wife, various Friends. No Maurice. Kitty accepted a glass of sherry and felt a momentary pang of fear. Not about the lecture: that was written down, and she would perform however badly she felt. But about these people who were to become her colleagues and associates and from whom she suddenly felt so estranged! Redmile chanting,

168

'Splendid! Splendid! Great stuff!' His disaffected secretary Jennifer, circulating with the standard bottle of sherry. The Roger Fry Professor's face getting too red too quickly. His wife, stoking up on peanuts. The high uninhibited voices of the Friends, none of whom appeared to know who Kitty was or what her function was. Their awful clothes, she thought. She stuck close to Pauline, not willing to launch herself into this alien sea until it had been sanctioned by Maurice. With Maurice there she would begin to revive.

Professor Redmile came over to them, one hand sweeping through his sparse but long hair. 'You will have a splendid audience, Miss Maule. Not nervous, I hope?' Suddenly, she was.

'I shall be quite relieved when it is over,' she smiled.

'Of course, of course. But if it will make you feel any better, I can tell you that there may be good things to follow. Of course, I cannot say anything yet. But I think you may feel confident. Ah, there is Maurice. I was beginning to think he had been detained.'

Maurice, unaccountably wearing a dinner jacket and looking extremely handsome, greeted several people, all of whom turned to him as he entered, abandoning their partners, spouses, and whatever they had been saying. Kitty, her face radiant with relief, ignored Pauline's warning glance and made as if to go over to him. But although he smiled at her, his eyes swept past her, and she was left standing expectantly and feeling rather alarmed. Why was he dressed? Where was he going? Why did she not know? She was aware of how little she knew about his life, and this knowledge was unwelcome at such a juncture, for she wanted to feel her new confidence, she wanted so much to enjoy her anticipation and for it to be unmarred.

Pauline, looking at her, said rather quickly, 'I think you may have to do something about Larter, Kitty.

He seems to have taken to you.'

'But his work is quite all right,' said Kitty, her eyes still shocked.

'He is apparently making rather a nuisance of himself in the town. When I say the town, I mean the bicycle factory again, and that awful caff near the station where the long-distance lorry drivers go. If you were to have a word with him? He wouldn't take it from us. He regards us as senior citizens, unacquainted with the joy of sex. As indeed some of us are,' she added, after a pause.

'I really don't think I can ... ' Kitty began, but at this point Professor Redmile came up to her, his geniality reinforced by the heat of the evening.

'When you are ready, Miss Maule. I shall introduce you very briefly. Good luck. Quite an ordeal for her,' he said, in much the same tone of voice, to the Friend on his left, as Pauline touched Kitty on the arm and nodded towards the door. Really, thought Kitty, momentarily nettled, I am not deaf. I am not incapable. I am even very slightly bored with this evening. I should like to be taken out to dinner afterwards, not go straight home, where Caroline will be waiting. 'Hello, Maurice,' she said with studied carelessness. 'You're surely not going to sit through this, are you? You will be bored to death.' He smiled at her as if he knew everything she was thinking and had been thinking since he had first come into the room. 'Of course I'm coming. Good evening, Pauline.' 'Good evening, Maurice,' said Pauline, her hand tightening on Kitty's arm as she urged her forwards. A surge of panic ripped through Kitty. I am not ready for this, she thought. It is not going to be quite as easy as I supposed. Her eyes looked back to where Maurice was standing, detained by a Friend. He winked at her over the Friend's head, and then she was all right again.

Standing on the rostrum, while Professor Redmile

began what he had described as a brief introduction and which somehow managed to incorporate a fairly dense account of the plans he had devised for the structure of the New Building, she felt quite composed. She managed to seem interested in what was said, although she could see the Roger Fry Professor's hand pressed to his brow in the front row. She was indeed alarmed by the fact that she could see and recognize so many people. Many, she knew from experience, were already sinking into a brief doze from which she might or might not be able to rouse them. Maurice, bless him, was near the door, where she could glance at him from time to time without appearing to do so. She began to feel something of a professional challenge; this had to be good. The room was surprisingly full, not only with students from the Romance Languages Department, but with the curious, who attended these special evening lectures rather as if they were bull fights or gladiatorial contests, to see if the performer were going to get hurt. It was murderously hot. As Professor Redmile appeared to be reaching some sort of conclusion satisfactory to himself, she straightened up, unclenched her fists, and cleared her throat. She allowed herself one more look at Maurice, and then caught sight of Larter, grinning in unashamed encouragement, his thumb jerking discreetly upwards. Kitty smiled, and when Professor Redmile turned to her, and she heard a small patter of applause, she was quite confident. 'Ladies and gentlemen,' she began, in her clear voice, 'I should like to examine, if I may, some aspects of the Romantic Tradition, a tradition which still affects us today, although we may not recognize it. For although we think we know what a Romantic is, Romantics do not always know it themselves.' There was a little murmur of laughter and the lecture had begun.

171

F I F T E E N

In extreme heat, and in the brilliant sunlight of early morning, Old Church Street bore a passing resemblance to a deserted Mediterranean port. Empty, silent, and sun-struck, the pavements were already dusty from the long drought. Leaning out of her window at seven o'clock on the Saturday morning, Kitty Maule could smell the river a hundred yards away: rank and insistent, for the water was low. The sun drained her of appetite, almost of thought, and she could not envisage the moment at which it would be evening, when the punishing glare would diminish, when a small crowd would gather on the pavement outside the pub and stay there, becalmed, in the warm milky air, until the light went altogether.

It seemed unnatural to dress in this weather and she contemplated staying indoors in her nightgown until it was time to prepare for the evening. But this was clearly inadmissible, and besides the extraordinary light had a peremptory appeal, as if she must go out into it and feel its strength, as if not to do so were some kind of perversion. All over England sensible people sat in the shade. Those intoxicated by the great sun innocently offered their faces and bodies to it, waiting to be transformed into something more than their habitual pale selves. With no garden of her own, Kitty was reduced to wandering along the bleached streets of her immediate neighbourhood or sitting in the small public square by the river. She dreaded this place for the memory it had left with her of that ancient mother and daughter, and also because Caroline tended to sit there, exuding discontent. Kitty's own serenity was powerful enough to survive intact until the evening, but she thought it a pity to let it get unnecessarily damaged. Nevertheless, she spent most of the morning in the garden.

There was much to think about. She found herself in the unaccustomed situation of being popular and successful. To her not very great surprise, she had passed the test of her lecture with flying colours. Coming home alone, afterwards, she had felt a sense of well-being and almost of worth; she was assured of a permanent post for next year and could thus conclude that her apprenticeship was at an end. For two days she had rested secure in this knowledge and also in anticipation of a pleasant future. Pleasant in the sense of corresponding to her modest worth; pleasant in the sense of its being the correct conclusion of her attempts to achieve a position that would somehow merge her anomalous beginnings into her stronger linguistic background; pleasant in the sense that at last she had a feeling of place and could connect herself with an institution in which her ambitions, which were as modest as her experience, could be and would be realized. This would be, as it were, her daytime self. For stronger emotions and delights, for a more positive future, she would place her faith in the events that would be brought to birth by Maurice's (and her) dinner party. For the first time in her life she felt nothing but confidence in the future.

The garden was deserted. Along the Embankment, lorries rumbled in the shimmering air; the sun was so strong that Kitty could hardly bear to read. At what she assumed was lunchtime, several men brought their glasses of beer down from the pub, loosened ties, and soon removed shirts altogether. Dazed, she stood up, aware that she must go home and eat something, and that more time had passed than she had accounted for. She wanted everything to be rational and measured today; she wanted to be as safely in control as she had been on that astonishing Tuesday; she wanted to be excellent. She brought bread and cheese and two peaches, and made some strong coffee, a little uncertain of what to do with the afternoon. Caroline was absent, to judge from the silence, although this was surely no weather for Harrods. 'What do you do there every day?' Kitty had asked her. Caroline had looked blank. 'But I don't go there every day. Sometimes I go to Harvey Nichols.' She had seemed to think this was a comprehensive answer. Suddenly Kitty missed her, would have welcomed the sound of Woman's Hour or some other soothing routine noise that would indicate the continuance of normal life. The silence was really rather alarming. She leaned out of the window again, as if she could summon up the apparition of Caroline on her way home, but the street was empty. Really, she thought, it is almost easier to be at work; I am not built for leisure. This heretical thought was soon dismissed to join others – a very slight boredom, an edginess, a certain low desire to show off in front of the Redmiles and the rest. As if a definite strategy were suddenly within her reach and could now be employed. As if her position might be strengthened by displaying what had been so sedulously concealed. There is really no need to conceal it any longer, she thought. In fact I shall lose face by further concealment, not the other way round. That is the paradox.

She poured herself the dregs of the coffee and was thankful that her sitting room lay in the shadow, that

174

the sun was on the windows directly opposite. She thought it might be politic to take a short rest, although she was already sharpened by impatience and anticipated triumph. It was not quite the innocent pleasure she had always felt before a party; it was complicated by the desire to impose herself as she had imposed herself on that hot evening in the crowded lecture hall. She placed her coffee cup on the bedside table, removed her dress, and lay down, glad now of the silence. Idly, she put out her hand to the books displaced by the coffee cup: a history of Gothic architecture, *Adolphe*, and Marie-Thérèse's Bible. They were suddenly devoid of virtue. Kitty smiled. They have seen me through, she thought; I shall not need them again. Thank You, she added, politely.

She must have slept, for her next clear thought was of the time, which she could no longer calculate. With wakefulness came a strange and unanticipated feeling of desolation, as if she would have been better employed in doing something sensible with the day instead of consecrating it to the evening. Distressed, she sat upright, hoping that she was not going to sink into the panic that sometimes overtook her without warning. She found herself worrying whether she would be able to eat, in this great heat, and the very reflection brought with it an echo of that terrible cry, 'Marie-Thérèse! Marie-Thérèse!' It was the source of all her woes. But that is over, she assured herself, struggling against despair. This panic is quite irrational, due to nothing more serious than discomfort and low blood sugar. Make tea, and after tea, go out and buy an evening paper. She followed her own advice as if it had been dictated by someone else, but noticed that the hand holding the cup was shaking very slightly.

It was better in the street. Patches of sweat showed across the back of the greengrocer's overall; children slumped in push-chairs, one finger in their mouths, returned to babyhood. It was easier to talk to strangers in the great heat, which struck up from the pavements and rushed by in waves from passing buses. Kitty found herself checking the time, as if calculating at what moment it would be suitable to go home and start preparing herself. For the moment she was unwilling to leave the hectic weary street, and wanted to be at one with ordinary people, not marked out for this great test or triumph, whatever it was to be. She wanted to be able to go home to an ordinary house after an ordinary day's work, to sit in a deck chair and eat something without worrying about it, to watch the light fade and die, and then to go indoors to an unremarkable bed, and the prospect of a night's sleep and another day just like the one that had already ended. But this is not to be my way, she thought. It seems that everything will be more difficult than I supposed.

As she let herself into her flat she heard the sound of the five o'clock news, and her relief that Caroline was there drove her previous distress to the very edges of her mind. Unprecedently, she rang Caroline's bell. When Caroline appeared, she was wearing an old paisley silk dressing gown that had once belonged to her husband and her face was puffy. 'Are you all right?' asked Kitty. 'I feel a bit off, actually,' Caroline replied. 'I was thinking of taking a couple of aspirin and going to bed. Have you got anything to read, Kitty?' Kitty found her some paperbacks and the latest *Vogue*, which she intended to take to her grandmother the following day. 'Do you need anything?' she asked. 'I shall be out later, you know, so think about it now.' 'Oh, yes,' said Caroline, patting down a yawn. 'Your boyfriend's dinner party. No, I don't want anything, thanks. Let me know how it went. I expect I shall be all right tomorrow. And thanks for the *Vogue*.' With which she made as if to shut the door, but Kitty, superstitiously, put out her hand, and said, 'Wish me luck!' 'Oh, really, Kitty, you don't need luck to go to a dinner party! Just think of me lying here. That should make you feel better.' And the door was closed.

She did not look all that well, thought Kitty. If she is really going down with something, I ought to stay. She looked at her watch; it was half-past five, and she was due at Maurice's house at half-past seven. I shall feel better after a bath, she thought. I might as well start getting ready; anything might happen at the last moment.

In the bath she tried to dismiss the realization that Caroline had not wished her luck. But had she not dismissed from her life all these signs and portents, all these omens, whether sanctified or not? Her search for corroborating evidence of the life to come she now saw as the rankest superstition, yet this in some strange way intensified her fear rather than lessening it. She doubted if she could ever manage to set foot inside a church again. For she felt herself to be more rigorously excluded than ever, and the fact that everything she had ever asked for had come about, more or less, in no way diminished the wariness that persisted in her relations with the unknown. She shrugged impatiently. I am like those awful people who win a large sum on the football pools and swear that it will not change their way of life. I do not deserve my luck. And I had better get a move on: it is ten to six.

Dressed, she felt calmer, more adult, more controlled. A taxi had been ordered from the local car hire firm the evening before, so there was nothing to do except wait. She sat at the window, as she had known she would, and tried to retrieve her keenness, her sense of the main chance, that brief moment of realism that would have to serve instead of simplicity and happiness. I am sorry, she

177

thought, and almost said the words: I should have liked to have enjoyed this more, to have been more worthy of the occasion, to have been up to Maurice's standards. It seems as if I am doomed to fall below them. Why should this be? She tried to summon up the image of Maurice, but it was so difficult when he was not there; for some reason, she had never been able to picture his face. She had no photograph of him and all she carried in her mind was a sort of outline, a silhouette, as if she were seeing him against the sun, and the occasional involuntary memory of an ear, a hand, the excluding smile. She wondered, again, where he had been going the other night, dressed in his dinner jacket. Perhaps his mother had been giving a dinner party and he had driven down for the lecture and was going to drive back again afterwards. His parents owned a house in Ebury Street, and Maurice had a rather large flat of his own in the basement. Some sort of family occasion, she supposed, before the parents departed again for Gloucestershire. She was wistful. She was as remote from such occasions as her grandmother had been from Glyndebourne. Yet Louise had always known what was required. There was no reason why she, Kitty, should not do the same.

One last look in the glass. She was looking well, or as well as she ever would. She was appropriately dressed. She was suitable. She heard the taxi winding down the street, slowing, stopping. She leaned out of the window and signalled that she would be down. As she locked her door, Caroline's door opened to reveal Caroline, a handkerchief pressed to her nose. 'What a time to get a cold,' she said, thickly. She looked older, almost plain. 'Good luck, Kitty. You look very nice. I probably shan't see you when you get back. You might give me a ring tomorrow.' 'Will I be all right?' asked Kitty. 'Oh, of course you will. What's the matter with you? Although

I still prefer the dress with my chains,' she added. It was a qualified blessing but it would have to do.

'Good evening, madame,' said the taxi driver. Oh, God. It was Old Haileyburian who sometimes drove her and who always lost the way and talked incessantly, over his shoulder, of the time when he had been a farmer in Zambia. 'Big night, tonight?' 'Good evening,' said Kitty. She was rather early and had thought of asking the man to drive around but now she was anxious to get rid of him. She would walk a little at the other end, take a few deep breaths, and pretend this was an evening just like any other. 'A dinner party,' she answered politely. 'Ebury Street, please.' He had had a few drinks, as usual, and the hot car smelt of whisky. 'I don't expect you'll be seeing me much longer,' he continued. 'Thinking of trying my luck out there again. Still have contacts, you know. Politics is the art of the possible, and all that. Know who said that?'

They drove slowly, but jerkily, along the King's Road while he expounded on his habitual theme. This country's finished. Nobody willing to do a day's work any more. Exports up the spout. Bloody foreigners everywhere. What this country needs. Stiff dose of unemployment. Someone like Churchill. I fancy Mrs Thatcher for a change. Couldn't do worse than this lot. Bloody unions buggering it all up, if you'll pardon my French. Kitty drew in her breath as the car shot past and nearly overturned a cyclist. 'Nervous?' he asked pleasantly, turning round to her, his arm on the back of the front seat. 'You seem unusually tense, if I may say so. And yet as lovely as ever.'

She swallowed. They were approaching the small triangle in Pimlico Road that marked the end of her territory and the beginning of Maurice's domain. Suddenly she felt exhilarated, shaky with excitement. 'Drop me here,' she said. 'I'd like to walk a little.' He drew up to the kerb with a flourish, opening her door at the same time. As they came to an abrupt halt, he surveyed her openly. 'Mind if I ask what all this is about?' he enquired, with sodden charm. 'Big night?' Kitty emerged from the car thankfully and breathed the stale evening air as if she were on the shore of a distant sea. 'Wish me luck,' she said, proffering two pounds. 'Oh, I do, I do,' he replied, stowing the money away in a bulging wallet. 'Well, if we don't meet again ... ' 'Oh, of course,' said Kitty. 'You're going back to Africa. Well, the very best of luck to you too.' She stood on the pavement and waved to him as he executed a dangerous turn and plunged back in the direction of Sloane Square.

When she had looked in a few shop windows and then decided to go straight to Maurice's and see if he wanted any help and had turned her steps resolutely to Ebury Street, she noted with a start that it was already half-past seven. She could feel the blood warm in her cheeks and her heart was beginning to pound. Maurice had told her to come straight down to the basement, where she would find the door open. She had only been to his house once before, shortly after their first meeting, when he had had a large party and she had just been one of the many guests. She was glad she had dismissed the taxi and was arriving on silent feet. She looked with love at the soft, bright evening, at the beautiful dirty city. Soon I shall be where I have always wanted to be, she thought, in his house. But I must be practical now. I am, after all, here in a very special capacity.

She heard a voice call her name and, turning back, was surprised to see John Larter, wearing a very tight snuff-coloured velvet suit. 'Why, John,' she exclaimed. 'How unusual to see you here. In London, I mean,' she added hastily. 'This is a bit of luck,' he grinned. 'I believe I am to take you in, as they say. I wondered if I should call for you at your flat, or whether we should amalgamate here.' 'Take me in?' asked Kitty. 'Yes, I was given to understand that we are sort of partners. At least, maybe I've got it all wrong. Professor Bishop told me to look after you. Maybe we are all supposed to look after you.' He laughed and passed a hand through his already untidy hair. 'How kind of you, John,' she said, and thought, how kind of Maurice. He truly wants it to be my evening.

They reached the door of Maurice's basement and voices were already raised on the other side of it. As they rang the bell, the door was flung open to reveal Professor Redmile in full spate. Lady Redmile, nodding and smiling, was seated on the sofa, and the Roger Fry Professor and his wife, quite clearly in the throes of some private argument, stood gazing into their glasses. No Maurice. Kitty drew a deep breath and greeted them, gazing round in delighted recognition at the dark red walls. Nothing had changed. There was evidence here of much greater wealth than was normally associated with university professors, and the Redmiles were thawing in the reflected glow, while the Roger Frys appeared to have been driven into permanent opposition. Professor Redmile, indeed, was so delighted with his surroundings that he acted as if he were entirely at home, pouring out the sherry, and lifting his glass to Kitty. 'We are celebrating,' he announced. 'Yes, we are celebrating two delightful pieces of news. Or perhaps three,' he amended. 'But I can't say anything about that until Maurice comes.' 'Where is Maurice?' asked Kitty. 'Oh, I believe he is in the kitchen with his helpmate,' replied Professor Redmile. 'Quite delightful, as ever. He has asked me to hold the fort. Well,' he continued, pouring out more sherry, and frowning slightly as Larter proffered his glass. 'We are celebrating, as I was saying, two delightful pieces of news. One is Miss Maule's appointment to our staff.' He raised his glass again.

181

'And the other,' he sounded even more lyrical, 'is Maurice's lamented, alas, lamented removal to Oxford. Yes,' he put up a hand as they murmured in surprise. 'Yes, of course I am sorry, but what a proud day for our university, and for Maurice himself.' Kitty felt cold. He did not tell me, she thought. The Roger Fry Professor cleared his throat. 'Does that mean we shall not have the pleasure of hearing him on the cathedrals of France?' he enquired. Kitty saw his wife kick him quite hard on the ankle. 'Oh, I have arranged that he should continue the evening lectures for as long as he can,' smiled Professor Redmile. 'We shall quite understand if the pressure of other business,' he twinkled, 'or indeed of other pleasure forces him to stop a little earlier than anticipated.' 'Yes, indeed,' said the Roger Fry Professor fervently. Larter, raising his eyes in despair, dropped all pretence and poured himself another drink. 'I wonder if Maurice needs any help,' murmured Kitty, half rising. 'No need to worry, my dear,' assured Professor Redmile. 'I was told by our host and hostess that they would join us as soon as they could.' At which point the door opened and Kitty at last saw Maurice, and with him Miss Fairchild, in her usual cotton skirt. She was carrying a large tureen of soup, and Maurice was steadying her with a hand in the small of her back. Larter quickly downed his drink as he saw Kitty's face. 'Come, Miss Maule,' boomed Professor Redmile, who had not seen anything, 'let me escort you.'

They took their places at the table, Maurice and Miss Fairchild at either end. I lacked the information, thought Kitty, trying to control her trembling hands. Quite simply, I lacked the information. She had the impression of having been sent right back to the beginning of a game she thought she had been playing according to the rules. And there was the rest of the evening to be got through. Professor Redmile was in ever more radiant form. 'I must confess, Miss Maule, that we were discussing you before you arrived. We were trying to work out which half of you was French.' The Roger Fry Professor's wife exploded into sudden high-pitched laughter. 'It was Kitty's mother,' supplied Maurice. 'Isn't that right, Kitty?' 'My father was in the army,' said Kitty Maule slowly. 'He died before I was born.' And picking up her spoon, she prepared to eat.

Anita Brookner's novels *The Debut* (published under the title *A Start in Life* in the United Kingdom) and *Look at Me* were critically acclaimed on both sides of the Atlantic. She is considered an international authority on eighteenth- and nineteenth-century painting and currently teaches at the Courtauld Institute of Art in London.